Maryelle peered through the soot-covered glass, hoping for some sign she would like this place.

Apart from a huddle of trees to the right, it was the same as the last dozen stops. But it wasn't buildings or scenery that brought her here; it was Kingston Brown, her husband. Her heart picked up its pace, and she smiled. She would have gone to the heart of darkest Africa if it meant she could be with Kingston. Would the war have changed him? Would he find her unsuitable now that they were in Canada, not London? Would their love be as strong and sure as she remembered it?

Suddenly, as she made her way to the door, she couldn't breathe. What if Kingston hadn't come? What if he'd changed his mind about her? About their love?

LINDA FORD draws on her own experiences living in the Canadian prairie and Rockies to paint wonderful adventures in romance and faith. She lives in Alberta, Canada, with her family, writing as much as her full-time job of taking care of a paraplegic and four kids who are still at home will allow. Linda says, "I thank God that He has given me a full, productive life and that I'm not bored. I thank Him for placing a little bit of the creative energy revealed in His creation into me, and I pray I might use my writing for His honor and glory."

Books by Linda Ford

HEARTSONG PRESENTS
HP240—The Sun Still Shines
HP268—Unchained Hearts
HP368—The Heart Seeks a Home
HP448—Chastity's Angel
HP463—Crane's Bride
HP531—Lizzie

Maryelle

Linda Ford

Heartsong Presents

Sometimes people come into our lives and give us a glimpse of an upbringing vastly different from the one we know. My friend, Steve, allowed me such glimpse which enabled me to write this book. It is to him I dedicate this story.

A note from the Author:
I love to hear from my readers! You may correspond with me by writing:

Linda Ford
Author Relations
PO Box 719
Uhrichsville, OH 44683

ISBN 1-58660-771-5

MARYELLE

PRINTED IN THE U.S.A.

one

March 1919
Alberta, Canada

"Next stop, Flat Rock," the conductor announced, pausing at Maryelle's side. "Your journey is almost over, Ma'am. I wish you all the best."

Maryelle sat up straighter, her chest impossibly tight as the train slowed and puffed to a halt. She leaned toward the window for a closer look.

"It's nothing much to look at, I'll grant you," offered the woman across the aisle. "But you'll find it a pleasant enough spot."

Maryelle peered through the soot-covered glass, hoping for some sign she would like this place. Apart from a huddle of trees to the right, it was the same as the last dozen stops. But it wasn't buildings or scenery that brought her here; it was Kingston Brown, her husband. Her heart picked up its pace, and she smiled. She would have gone to the heart of darkest Africa if it meant she could be with Kingston. Would the war have changed him? Would he find her unsuitable now that they were in Canada, not London? Would their love be as strong and sure as she remembered it?

Suddenly, as she made her way to the door, she couldn't breathe. What if Kingston hadn't come? What if he'd changed his mind about her? About their love?

She'd heard of other Canadian soldiers who had found solace

in the arms of English girls during the war, even married them, only to abandon them when they returned to home soil. She and Lizzie, her traveling companion, had been inundated with stories from both sides of the coin. Their trip had seemed interminably long, but Maryelle wished now she'd had more time to prepare herself for this reunion.

"Ma'am?" The conductor reminded her he was still waiting for her to step down.

"Yes, of course," she murmured.

She glanced up and down the platform and saw Kingston immediately. She would have recognized him anywhere. Tall and slender, straight as a rod, exactly as she remembered him. He hadn't seen her as he hurried along the platform checking in the car windows. And then his gaze slid to her; their eyes met; the air sucked from her lungs.

His blue-green eyes were exactly as she remembered—as mercurial as the Mediterranean Sea.

He took three quick steps. "Maryelle."

At the sound of his voice, rough with emotion, she dropped her bag and flung herself into his arms. The two-year separation was over. She had come home.

He swept her off her feet.

They clung together in an embrace that threatened to crush her ribs, but she welcomed the assurance he was here and still wanted her. She tipped back her head to drink in the sight of him.

"My brown-eyed English miss. I thought you'd never get here." She knew he didn't mean the late arrival of the train; he referred to the endless separation of the past two years since he'd been shipped to France and then home.

"Let me look at you." His eyes flashed so green she smiled.

"Mr. Canada, your eyes are turning green."

"It must be the trees."

She gave a joyful little laugh. It was a little game they'd played. She said she could always tell his mood by the color of his eyes. And he insisted they only reflected his surroundings, not his feelings. "There are no leaves on the trees yet."

"Then it's the grass."

There was no grass within a hundred feet. Her laugh was smothered by his kisses. She clung to him, letting his firm mouth cleanse her of the pain and fear of the last two years.

"Your bags, Ma'am."

She jerked back, her cheeks burning as she remembered how public their reunion was.

The man chuckled. "Don't let me interrupt. You go right ahead and let this young man know how much you missed him."

To her utter surprise and amazement, a sob shuddered through her, and tears gushed from her eyes.

"Oh, sweet Maryelle, don't cry," Kingston crooned, pressing her face into his coat front.

She wrapped her arms around him and hung on like a drowning person to a life preserver. Kingston stroked her hair and cradled her close. She tried to stop the flow, but her worry and loneliness had been bottled up too long and would not be controlled.

"Let's get out of here." Kingston edged her to a wooden wagon bench and climbed up beside her.

With one last shuddering sigh against his chest, Maryelle stopped crying. "I want to see what Flat Rock looks like." She hiccoughed.

Kingston laughed. "Then you best sit up and take notice

real quick. No wait—I have a better idea. I'll turn around, and we'll take the grand tour."

Pressed to his side, she dashed away her tears.

A long row of small frame buildings lined either side of a wide dusty street. Rough wooden signs with the name of the business swung gently. A collection of wooden houses surrounded the shops until the open land absorbed the town.

"It's not London," Kingston said.

She thought of the stately brick buildings, the lovely old cathedrals, the never-ending city, and the crowds of people. "I'd say it's not, but I like the open spaces. Reminds me of the trips Dad and I would take into the country. I always loved those trips."

At the mention of her father, Kingston's arm tightened around her.

She gave a shaky sigh, but now was not the time for sadness. She was home at last, and she immediately loved Kingston's country.

They took a side street out of town.

"My sweet Maryelle," Kingston whispered. "You're even prettier than I remember you."

"And I'm thinking that the war must have damaged your eyesight."

He laughed. "Still the saucy miss too."

"I've never been saucy," she protested. "I can't help it if I happen to know my own mind."

"I'm glad you do." He grew still. She tipped her head to study him. Worry, like pinpricks, trickled up her spine at the serious look in his dark green eyes. Finally he said, "And I'm hoping you're as sure about how you feel about me as you were in London."

She choked back a sob; she would not cry again, but she hadn't imagined Kingston being as fearful as she about whether or not their love had survived the war. It gave her a sense of sureness. Grinning so wide her eyes stung, she hugged him. "Kingston Brown, I love you as much now as I did when we married—no, a thousand times more."

"Ah, my sweet Maryelle. How glad I am to hear that." He smiled at her in a way that made her insides tingle. "Now tell me everything."

During her two months of travel, they'd been unable to communicate. "You and this other war bride were able to travel together?" At her nod, he sighed. "I was so relieved to know you wouldn't be alone. What was she like?"

"Lizzie? A sweet, gentle young woman from a close family. I think she's going to miss them very much. I wanted to see her husband; but with all the delays, we got there in the middle of the night. I'll have to wait for her letter to hear how things went."

"Maryelle, my lovely, I know you've left behind everything dear and familiar to you, but I promise I'll do my best to make up for it." He pulled her back to his chest. "I hope it will be enough."

His eyes flashed the color of sun-kissed water, making her forget everything but her love for him. She wrapped her arms around him and squeezed. "It's been so long. There were times I wondered if I'd ever see you again. It's a miracle you survived the war—that I survived." Before he had been shipped to France, they'd had four days of honeymoon bliss and, before that, weeks of companionable courting, and now she had him to hold again.

"Praise God we did. And now it's over, and we can build our lives together. You and I are part of the new future.

But first things first." He pulled the wagon under the shelter of some barely budded trees and tied the reins. "I have missed you every minute of every day." He buried his fingers in her hair. "My Maryelle, sweetest rose that ever bloomed."

Kingston, with his sweet talk, had always filled her heart with gladness. She didn't realize how much she'd missed it, having locked it away to keep from drowning in her loneliness; but, suddenly released, her need for it leapt into a yawning abyss that almost frightened her. She wasn't sure she could control the love flooding her heart. "I have missed you beyond reason," she said before he finally kissed her. She wanted to hold him forever.

Kingston cupped her face in his hands. "Let's walk for a bit. I'm determined to hear what's happened since I last heard from you." He jumped from the wagon and lifted her to the ground. His gaze went up and down her length, finally resting on her face.

Maryelle saw his eyes had grown as dark as pine needles.

"You're all in one piece, I see."

"You expected me to arrive in bits and pieces?"

"No, miss smarty pants." He sobered. "But a lot of people have changed drastically. I know things got tough in Britain. I guess I was afraid you'd suffer. You probably did, but it doesn't show—on the outside at least."

She laughed. "I will take that as a compliment." Perhaps they'd talk about the past later or perhaps not.

"It's a mighty poor compliment for someone as fine looking as yourself, but it is a compliment nevertheless." He grabbed her hand and led her along a grassy path. "I assure you there will be more and better compliments to follow."

"Kingston, how has it been since you came home?" She'd only had one letter since he returned to Canada, six weeks before she began her journey to join him. "Is everything as you expected? Are you happy? Why didn't you write more often? I could get your letters right up until I left. I worried things had changed—between us." She gulped back the fears that wouldn't be quieted even by having his arm around her shoulders.

He paused beneath a lone sprawling tree with feathery seed clusters hanging like fine old lace and pulled her under the dangling branches, leaning against the trunk, his booted leg tipped against the bark.

Maryelle's chest tightened with loving him. He was so handsome with his reddish brown hair—the color of old brick, she'd once told him—and his unusual eyes—Canada green, she'd dubbed them.

He looked so relaxed. There had always been something about him—the way he moved and the way he spoke—that said he was comfortable in his life.

"I'm extremely happy to be home. I'll admit it's hard to settle back into civilian life after being in the trenches in France." He shrugged. "Sometimes it's hard to decide which is reality—the war or now."

"The war is something that will always have had a hand in the shape of our lives. I'm thankful it is finally over. I hope I never hear another siren as long as I live." A shudder snaked across her shoulders. "And those horrible silver cigars." She used the name many used to describe the German zeppelins that had threatened London.

"The war to end all wars." He took her hands. "Thank the Lord both of us survived that and the flu epidemic."

"And the farm?" It had been his goal post while he fought in the mud and disease of the trenches.

"The farm is still here."

"You expected it to move?"

He tweaked her nose. "I suppose I wondered if there would be a place for me when I got back. After all, Dad managed without me for three years."

"So, in your wonderfully illuminating way, you're telling me you've found you're still needed on the farm?"

"You've guessed it right. How keen of you."

She laughed. "Have I told you how much I missed you?"

"I don't believe you have." He caught her chin and tipped her head back. "But me first. Let me show you how much I've missed you." He bent and captured her lips again with gentleness. When he would pull away, she wound her hands around his neck and would not let him go.

Laughing, he said, "Isn't this a lot better than a bunch of sweet words?"

"I'll take both."

He sank to the ground, his back against the tree, and pulled Maryelle to his lap. He kissed her nose. "You are my sweet English rose, fairest bloom that ever grew." He kissed her eyelids. "You are my sunshine and my sky." He pressed ten kisses to her temple, then trailed more down her cheeks, and buried several under her chin. "Light of my life, joy of my heart, sweetness of my soul." He lifted his head, cradling her face in his palms. "Maryelle Brown, my wife and my joy, I love you."

Her throat tightened. How she loved this man who seemed to have no limit to the number of ways he found to express his love. She wished she could be so articulate with her own feelings, but her emotions swelled inside her rather than flooding out as did his. She pressed her open palms to his shoulders as if the action would somehow let her emotions flow from her heart to his. "Kingston Brown, my dear and lovely husband, I love you more than anything, including life. I will do my very best to make you happy."

"I can't imagine being any happier than I am right now. It's like getting married all over." His kiss was sweet and gentle.

She would have stayed pressed to his chest all day, but Kingston shifted. "I suppose we should go home. My family is eager to meet you, and there's always work to be done. I sometimes think Dad saved it for me the whole time I was gone."

At the mention of his family, she jerked upright. "Ah, into the lions' den. Best get it over with." She laughed in an attempt to remove the sting from her words, but inwardly she wondered how his family would take to her. Would they resent her as an outsider? Or welcome her with open arms? "How much farther?"

He scrambled to his feet, pulling her up. "It's not far."

"Seems 'not far' is a favorite expression of you Canadians, and it can mean anything from a five-minute walk to a four-day ride on a fast horse. Why didn't you tell me Canada was so big?"

"I tried, but it's hard for anyone to understand. It's another five miles or so."

"I guess I'll get used to the distances."

"No doubt you'll find lots of things you'll have to get used to."

She tugged his hand, forcing him to stop and look at her. "That sounds dreadfully ominous. Are you trying to warn me of something?"

"Of course not." He laughed and stroked his finger down her nose. "I only mean everything will seem different to you.

You've always lived in a big city. Now you'll be living on a farm. Your country is old with tons of history. Canada is new and fresh. We're still writing our history." He shrugged. "It's a lot different."

"I like that, 'writing our history.' "

He lifted her arm and twirled her around. "That's you and me, Mrs. Brown. We've just begun to write our history together. We've a whole lifetime of discovery ahead of us." He draped an arm across her shoulders. "Together forever, you and me."

"Have I told you how much I missed you, Mr. Brown?"

He tightened his arm around her. "Not in almost five minutes."

&

Kingston pulled the wagon to a halt on a small hill. "There it is, dead ahead. Your new home."

Maryelle clutched his arm and studied the buildings several hundred yards away—a two-story rambling house surrounded by trees, a hip-roofed red barn, and several smaller buildings scattered around the yard. Through the distance she heard a childish voice calling.

"My new home." Suddenly the enormity of the step she was about to take shook her. She faced Kingston. "My hair. It must be all tossed up." She dug a brush from her bag and struggled to pin the loose strands back into place. "How does it look?"

He grinned. "You look delightful, delicious, and totally desirable."

"Exactly how I want to look meeting your family for the first time."

He grabbed her in a crushing hug. "Exactly how I want you to look for me every day."

"Be serious." She pushed him away. "I don't want your parents to think I'm some English tart. Is my hair tidy?"

"I suppose you're right. Here." He took the brush from her hand. "Let me fix it."

She turned on the seat so he could brush the strands into place and pin them. This side of Kingston had surprised her at first, his casualness at doing things she would have privately considered female, but how she'd missed it.

"I'd forgotten how good you are at this." Her voice quivered as his touch turned her bones to warm wax.

He dropped the brush in her lap and kissed her neck. She leaned into his chest, enjoying the way his breath tickled the curve of her neck. "It has been too long."

He turned her so he could look into her face. "My beautiful brown-eyed love. I'd like to take you away and have you all to myself for the rest of our lives." He sighed. "But as that isn't possible, what do you say about us getting ourselves home?"

"I'd like to say I've changed my mind. I prefer your idea. Let's run away to the mountains or the beach or wherever you Canadians run away to. But, as you say, that's not about to happen so"—she turned to face forward—"lead on. To whatever lies ahead."

She stiffened her backbone—after all, she wasn't British for nothing. A stiff upper lip and calm courtesy had seen many a Brit through a difficult time. But before she had time to fill her lungs adequately, Kingston pulled up before the house.

"Here we go," he murmured as he lifted her down.

"Death or victory," she vowed, repeating one of the cries of the British during the war.

"I hope it won't be that bad." Kingston laughed. "Let's go inside."

She nodded. In truth, if an escape had offered itself at that point, she knew she would have taken it.

He led her through a small, cluttered entryway into a large, overly warm kitchen. Strange faces and the smells of cooking food—turnips, potatoes, and fried meat—surrounded her. Despite her nervousness, her mouth watered.

Kingston pulled her to his side. "Maryelle, this is my family."

She blinked. There seemed to be so many of them.

"Mother, this is my wife."

Maryelle focused on this woman who had given Kingston life—heavyset; hazel eyes, much darker than Kingston's; and an unsmiling expression. "I'm so pleased to meet you," Maryelle said and held out her hand.

Kingston's mother wiped her hands on her apron as if to indicate they were far too dirty to be shaking hands with this stranger. Instead she gave a quick nod.

"Pleased to meet you." Her expression remained unchanged.

Maryelle ran her hand over her hair. Was it all tossed about? She traced her finger over her cheeks. Was her face dirty? "What would you like me to call you?"

"Mrs. Brown will do just fine."

Kingston's hand dropped to the back of her neck, his warm touch fortifying her.

"This is my father." She faced the older man, not as tall as Kingston, but heavier built. His eyes were deep blue.

"You can call me Dad." He took her hands in both of his. "So you're the young miss who stole my son's heart?"

"I'd say it was the other way around." Her heart rebelled at calling another man Dad, the loss of her own parents still too fresh. She'd call them Father and Mother Brown.

Kingston drew her farther into the room. "I'll start at the

top and work down. This is my sister, Lena, two years younger than me."

"That would make you twenty," Maryelle murmured.

Lena's gaze was fierce. "That's right." She turned away without saying hello.

"Next sister in line is Katherine, who is, what, sixteen?"

"I'm seventeen now," she informed Kingston. Then to Maryelle she said, "Hello."

For a moment Maryelle thought she caught an uncertainty in Katherine's expression. Who could blame her? Despite her marriage to their brother, Maryelle was a total stranger.

"And this strapping young lad of almost fifteen is my brother, Angus."

Angus kept his face down, hiding behind a mop of brown hair.

"Angus," his father said. "Speak to the young lady."

The boy jerked his head up, mumbled, "Hello," and ducked away again.

Kingston's touch on her neck grew firmer.

"And these are the little ones. My youngest sisters. Come on, girls—say hello to Maryelle."

Two little girls stepped forward, holding hands.

"Jeanie is six years old."

The child said, "Hello." Maryelle decided this child was most like her mother—brown hair, hazel eyes, a round face, and a steady, unblinking look.

"And this is Lily, who is five."

"Well, Lily, I'm pleased to meet you." This child had the reddish hair and blue-green eyes of her eldest brother as well as his warm gaze.

The child regarded her with curiosity. "We thought you was never going to get here. What took you so long? Kingston's been home lots of time already."

Lena squeezed Lily's shoulder. "Don't ask so many questions."

Maryelle laughed. "I don't mind."

Lena scowled.

Maryelle dropped her gaze to the child. "I thought it was a long time too."

"So did I," Kingston added. "Way, way too long."

"Dinner's ready and waiting," Mother Brown announced.

Kingston drew Maryelle to a chair at his side, taking her hand and holding it in his lap as they sat down. She clung to his strength. Everything was so strange. Even the meals had different names—dinner in the middle of the day!

She took a slow breath. Everything was strange—everything but Kingston. With him at her side, she could face anything. She would learn to know his family, and they, her.

Father Brown said a blessing, and the food was passed.

Maryelle stared at the abundance, mounds of boiled potatoes, a full bowl of cooked carrots, thick slices of fried pork. It had been months since she'd had more than a sliver of meat. "These potatoes are so nice and white. The ones we get this time of year are full of black mold." She took a mouthful of carrots. "And what lovely carrots. So sweet and fresh."

"We grow them ourselves. These are out of the root cellar." It was Kingston who answered her. He turned to the rest of the family. "I told you how Maryelle owned a green grocer's shop in London. She is very astute about vegetables."

"What's a green grocer shop?" Lily demanded.

"A shop—" Maryelle began.

"Store," Kingston explained.

Maryelle smiled at him. "Yes, a store where one sells vegetables and produce."

"Oh." The child tilted her head. "How come you talk so funny?"

The other girls tittered.

"Girls," Father Brown warned. "Mind your manners, hear?"

"Yes, Sir," Lena answered, her tone indicating she wasn't one whit sorry.

"Have some bread." Kingston held a plate toward her heaped with light, golden slices.

Maryelle turned a piece over and over. "How fortunate that the baker can still get such lovely flour." She felt every eye upon her.

Lena snorted. "We make it ourselves."

Maryelle tried again. "How lovely. Could you teach me how?"

"I'm sure someone will be glad to teach you." Kingston draped his arm across the back of her chair. "Right, Mom?"

His mother regarded him across the table. "It's not something one learns overnight."

"I'm a quick learner," Maryelle said.

"She surely is," Kingston said.

She ducked her head and ate in silence, feeling as if she'd been spit out and washed up on foreign shores.

"We'll be fixing the loft floor this afternoon," Father Brown announced, a few minutes later. "That is, if Kingston thinks he can tear himself away from his wife."

Kingston straightened and faced his dad. "I'll be out as soon as I take Maryelle's luggage to our room."

Father Brown's announcement signaled the end of mealtime. The girls sprang to their feet, and each gathered an armload of dishes.

Following their example, Maryelle piled plates. Lena took the dishes from Maryelle's hands. "No need for you to get your hands dirty."

"I want to help."

Father Brown had already ducked out the door, Angus hard on his heels. Kingston called over his shoulder, "I'll be back in a few minutes and show you our room."

Maryelle stood alone, facing one fierce young woman.

two

Maryelle realized at once that Lena had determined to make her unwelcome. A glance at Katherine convinced her the younger sister took her lead from the elder. She could expect no kindness from either of them.

She glanced at Mother Brown, her back turned as she washed dishes. Whether she was aware of the situation and chose to ignore it, Maryelle could not tell.

"I'm used to work," Maryelle explained. "I worked in the shop since I was a child and have run it on my own since Dad was killed in the war. I cared for my mother until she died." She swallowed back tears. The pain of losing them both was still unbearable at times. "I think I've managed quite well."

"That was there. This is here."

Maryelle drew back at the venom in Lena's voice.

"We got no need of a fancy English girl here."

"I'm no such thing. I'm a working girl." She struggled to remain calm, certain she had faced and dealt with more hardships than Lena. "I'd like to help."

Katherine watched, waiting, Maryelle was certain, to see who would be the victor in this struggle of the wills; but now Maryelle was also aware of two little girls peering at them. She had no wish to upset the young ones. "I'm sure there's some way I can help." She stepped back, dropping her hands to her side, but her retreat was only temporary. She had not gone through four years of war, hearing over and over the cry "death or victory" for nothing. But one worrisome thought wouldn't be ignored. Would the love Kingston and she shared survive a battle on the home front?

Kingston returned to the kitchen, one of Maryelle's trunks hoisted to his shoulder. "Come on. I'll take you upstairs."

She scurried after him, grateful for the diversion and equally eager to see their quarters.

Kingston clumped up the stairs, grunting under the load. She had a glimpse of several rooms as she followed him to the far end of the hall. Her heart turned to stone. Kingston had told her they'd be living with the family; yet somehow she'd envisioned a little flat of their own.

He pushed open the door, heaved the trunk to the floor, and stepped back, wiping his brow. "What did you bring, bricks?"

"No bricks. Sold them all before I came."

The room was tiny with a bed shoved under a sloping roof. There'd barely be room for her to unpack her things. She crossed to the window and looked down on the hills and the road.

Kingston swung her around. "My sweet brown eyes, I know this is hard. You've left everything to come here, and this is all I have to offer you."

"As long as we're together, everything will be all right." Hadn't she promised herself she would face fire, flood, dangers from man or beast, anything, to be with her beloved? Their two-year separation had taught her that.

But I didn't expect to encounter resistance from his family.

"I want to see if everything has arrived safely." She knelt before the trunk and unlocked the latches. After throwing the lid back, she unfolded the heavy coat on top to reveal a row of pictures, all intact. She lifted one, running her fingers around the silver frame. "It's Dad." She held it for Kingston to see.

He sprawled on the floor, head close to her side, legs almost under the bed.

"In his uniform just before he shipped out." She stroked the glass covering his likeness. "It was the last time I saw him." She pressed the picture to her chest.

Kingston kissed her. "I wish I could kiss away the hurt of losing him, but I've seen enough death to know I can't."

She leaned against him. "Nothing will ever take away the pain, though already I find it doesn't strike me as often and as hard as it did at first."

"That's as it should be." He settled back, waiting.

She put aside the picture. Later she would find a place to display it. The next picture was her mother. "I put the rest in an album, but this one is so beautiful I had it framed. I'll put Mom's and Dad's pictures next to each other."

Kingston leaned over and studied the picture. "She's beautiful."

"It was taken very long ago. I think it was about the time she and Dad married." Maryelle shrugged. "Before she began to age, before she gave up on life."

"I can sympathize with how she felt. If anything happened to you, I think I would want to curl up and die."

Maryelle nodded. "Seemed the life just seeped out of her after Dad's death."

He rubbed her shoulder. "It's hard for me to think of you going through the death of both your parents before I met you. I wish I could have been there to comfort you." His eyes were as green as a shadowed lake.

She leaned down and kissed him. "Mr. Canada, your eyes are changing color again."

"That's 'cause I'm feeling so bad for you." He lingered over the kiss.

She broke away. "Don't you want to see what other pictures I've brought?"

"This is much more fun."

She kissed his nose, then reached for another photo. "You and I on our wedding day." He had never seen it before and practically snatched it out of her hand.

"Well, aren't we the handsome couple though?"

"And truly modest too."

"I expect no one else will tell us how great we are so we might as well tell ourselves because, Mrs. Brown"—he leered into her face—"we are definitely great. Just look at us."

Their foreheads touched as they bent over the photo.

"You were so handsome in your uniform."

He jerked back. "You mean I'm not in my farm clothes?"

She giggled. "You'd be handsome in a sack."

"I never thought of it. I'll run right out and find me a sack and see if you're right."

"I'm sure I'd be very impressed."

"You would be." He waggled his eyebrows.

She turned back to the picture. "Doesn't it seem like a very long time ago?"

"Being apart seemed like a very long time." He took her face in his hands. "I'll never be apart from you like that again, God willing."

She kissed his forehead. "Have I told you how much I missed you?"

He put the picture on the floor beside the others so he could pull her into his arms. "My sweet wife, why is it I get the feeling that you really missed me?"

"Funny how you pick up on things so quickly." It felt so good to be in his arms, to feel the rise and fall of his chest, to hear the steady beat of his heart against her cheek. He rested his chin against her head, his fingers twined into her hair. Finally, with a deep sigh, she pushed away. "I have one more picture I want to show you." She reached around him and pulled it from the trunk. Without looking at it, she handed it to him.

He hooted with laughter. "Sheba. I can't believe you found a picture of her and framed it."

"Well, I miss her. She was my friend almost all my life."

"Maryelle, I don't know if you noticed, but Sheba was a cat."

She straightened and looked at him in pretend shock. "You don't say."

He chortled. "A big, furry, lazy, good-for-nothing cat."

"You only knew her when she was old. She wasn't always so lazy. In fact, she used to play some wild games of cat and mouse with me." She grinned. "Or perhaps I should say cat and girl."

"Still just a cat," he teased.

She snatched the picture from him. "Not just a cat. Not to me." Tears welled up. She sniffed. "I still miss her." Her voice quivered.

Kingston grabbed her chin and forced her to meet his gaze. "Are you crying?" There was no hiding the moisture in her eyes. He crushed her to him. "You know I was only teasing."

She let herself go limp against him.

He placed the picture beside the others. "Sheba shall have her place of honor with the rest of the family."

A giggle tickled the back of her throat. "She'd expect it."

Feeling better, she sat up. "Don't I have another trunk?"

He made a face and scrambled to his feet. "I'll go get it, your highness."

As he left, Maryelle sat back on her heels, cradling the pictures in her lap as if somehow she could hold the past as a shield against the present. She'd dreamed of the day she'd be with Kingston again, but never had she imagined she wouldn't be welcomed in his home.

The aloneness she felt now was worse than what she felt that day Kingston stepped into the shop in London seeking shelter from the cold rain. He'd walked into her life when she felt abandoned by her parents and by God. Kingston brought new meaning to her life. He'd filled the empty spots with his love.

She heard his steps thumping up the stairs and dashed away her tears. There was no need to feel alone. She had Kingston.

He lowered the second trunk to the floor. "More bricks?" he teased.

"China. I packed Mother's bone china. I hope it survived the trip." She threw back the lid, folded back the blankets, and unwrapped the top plate. "It's intact." She unwrapped several more pieces. "Oh, good. I think it's all fine."

Kingston dropped down at her side, lounging on one arm so he could examine her face. "The question I have is, are you okay?"

She rubbed her arms and patted her legs. "I seem to be."

"That's not what I mean."

"Then you had better tell me what it is you do mean."

His expression serious, he said, "I mean about living with my family."

"You told me what to expect, so why would I be surprised?" Only she was. She thought they'd have more rooms; that she would be made to feel welcome.

He grimaced. "How could I tell you what to expect when I didn't know myself? I saw the way you were treated." He grabbed her arm. "Don't you think I was hurt?"

Her heart went to him. He deserved better—so much better. "I suppose it will take time," she soothed. "I was rather looking forward to sharing your family. I've been so lonely since Mother passed away." She trailed her finger down his long nose. "Back home you taught me how to love and trust again. It seems so long ago, so far away. I guess you'll have to teach me all over again."

"Of course I'll help." He clasped her hand. "One thing I learned in the trenches—when everything seems dark and futile, there is still one place to turn: to God. If only we learned to turn there first, we'd save ourselves many heartaches."

His words sifted through her troubled emotions. "Together, with God's help, we'll make this work."

He pulled her into his arms, and the rise and fall of his chest rocked her gently.

"Maybe I haven't done the right thing bringing you here."

She jerked up and faced him. "Are you saying you should have left me in London?" She tucked in her chin. "Because if you are, I think you would find I had something to say about it. I would have come and found you one way or another."

"No, Silly." Ignoring her resistance, he pulled her back to

his chest. "I mean maybe I should have found us a place to rent in town."

There was no mistaking the pain in his voice as he uttered the words, and she hugged him tight. "Oh, Kingston, I know how much you love this farm, how much you missed it."

"I guess you should. I'm sure it was all I ever talked about or wrote about."

"Almost." She snuggled against him. "That's why you can count on me to make sure this works."

She felt the tension drain from him as he buried his face in her hair. "Mrs. Brown, I love you. Did you know that?"

"I won't expect you to remind me too often—no more than ten or twelve times a day."

He laughed softly against her hair. "I'll try to remember that."

Weariness overtook Maryelle. It had been a long trip. She could gladly fall asleep in his arms, but he shifted.

"I have to go help fix the loft."

"Not even one day for ourselves?"

"Dad will be expecting me to help." He sounded half asleep himself.

"Umm. I suppose."

They breathed gently in unison.

"What will I do while you're working?" Her eyelids were heavy.

He tried to sit up, but she slumped against him. "Looks to me like you need a nap."

"I'm feeling a bit fatigued." It seemed her head had grown too heavy for her neck. "I'd really cherish a bath though. Where is the bathroom?"

He chuckled. "There is the outhouse out back."

Having already encountered the accommodations he spoke of, she wrinkled her nose. "But where could I bathe?"

"In a big galvanized tub." He grinned at her.

"Sounds wonderful."

"First, you have to haul it in and up the stairs if you want to bathe in the privacy of our room. Then you have to heat water and haul it up."

Her mouth hung wide.

His eyes flashed a vivid blue-green. "Then when you're done, you haul it all out."

"You think I'm naive enough to believe that?"

"I'm not pulling your leg. It's the truth."

"I suppose that makes a bath impossible then?"

He gently held her as he stood to his feet. "For now. But I'll see that you get your bath this evening."

"I'm awfully tired."

He practically dragged her to bed. "I'll explain to Mother that you're resting." He pulled a quilt around her shoulders.

"Umm." Somehow she didn't think it would matter to Mother Brown or the girls that she wouldn't be around to help for a little while. "I'll be down as soon as I wake up."

"Rest well, my sweet Maryelle." He chuckled. "See now. I'm a poet, and I didn't know it." He pressed a kiss to her cheek and left the room.

❧

When she awoke, she bolted upright in bed. She'd dreamed she was with Kingston. She glanced around the strange room and remembered where she was. Being with Kingston was now more than a dream that ended with the morning light. How wonderful.

From outside came the sound of hammering; from below, the faint murmur of voices. She flung herself back on the pillow. This was not the reality she had imagined. If only it could be just her and Kingston. If only she didn't have to go down and face his family.

But Kingston wanted to be here. She crawled from bed, found the mirror over the dresser, and tidied her hair. With a deep breath to fortify herself, she headed for the stairs.

The murmur of voices stopped the minute she stepped into the room. She ground to a halt as three pairs of eyes stared at her—Lena at the table peeling potatoes, Katherine holding a sock to darn, Mother Brown rolling out dough at the end of the table.

"What can I do to help?" Maryelle asked.

Mother Brown turned her attention back to the dough, cutting it into neat diamond shapes; Katherine busily weaved her needle in and out. Only Lena returned her look, dark hazel eyes snapping, mouth tight and drawn up like a prune.

"I am perfectly capable, you know. I managed to run a business in London, after all."

Lena sniffed. "This is not the big city. We do things differently here."

Maryelle bit her bottom lip to keep from saying that rudeness to guests seemed one thing they did differently. But she wasn't a guest, she reminded herself. She was family now, and somehow she had to find a way of proving herself to these women. "Surely there's something I can do."

"Mom, see what I found." Lily raced across the kitchen

and plunked a furry branch on the table. "There's a bunch of them on the tree at the end of the road."

"Pussy willows," Mother Brown said. "Put them in a jar of water if you want to keep them."

Lily filled a jar with water. "I like pussy willows."

"What have you two been up to?" Lena demanded of Jeanie, who was following in Lily's trail.

"Nothing."

Lily bounced around, her Kingston-like eyes darting from one person to the next. "We were 'sploring. Maybe we'll find some kittens or baby birds."

Lena shook her head. "It's too early. The snow has barely left."

Jeanie lifted one shoulder. "Told ya."

"Don't care," the little one said, jamming her pussy willows in the jar.

Maryelle smiled at the stubborn cheerfulness of the child. She couldn't help wondering if Kingston had been like her when he was small.

Lena dumped the peelings into a bucket. "Here—take these to the chickens and check to see if there're any eggs."

Lily took the pail and rocked from one foot to the other. "She come?" She tipped her head toward Maryelle.

Lena's eyes narrowed. "Sure. Take her with you."

Maryelle met the older girl's look, knowing Lena meant to put her in her place. But she didn't care. Anything was better than feeling like an unwelcome intruder. She held Lena's gaze long enough to let her know she wasn't accepting defeat before she followed the child.

"Put on your coat," Mother Brown called.

Maryelle grabbed her own coat from the hook as Lily pulled on hers.

The little girl skipped ahead, swinging the pail in a wide arc. Jeanie stayed at Maryelle's side, studying her. Maryelle ignored her scrutiny and focused on the bright-spirited child ahead.

"Angus says we'll have baby everythings pretty soon," Lily announced over her shoulder.

"Baby what?"

Lily paused, the pail still for an instant. "Baby chicks, baby calves—we already got one—baby birds." She paused as if reciting a memorized list. "Oh, yeah. Baby geese, baby crows, baby robins." She took a deep breath, her face brightening. "And our horse, May, is going to have a colt." She resumed skipping, singing, "Babies, babies everywhere."

A tattered calico cat ran under the fence and wrapped itself around Lily's legs. The child paused to pet it. "Nice momma cat." She tipped her head up to study Maryelle. "You like cats?"

Maryelle stroked the cat meowing up at her. "I love cats, though I haven't known too many—just one special one."

"One? She was yours?"

"She was mine." Maryelle smiled at the memories of that one special cat. "My dad gave her to me when I was six years old, and she was my best friend. I used to dress her up, and she'd have tea with me."

Lily's eyes grew round. Jeanie inched closer.

"She slept with me every night as long as she lived."

Lily's mouth dropped open. "Your dad let her sleep with you?"

"He did."

Lily turned her wide eyes to her sister. "I'm going to ask my dad."

"You better not." Jeanie shook her head. "He doesn't like cats."

"I know." Her little shoulders sagged.

"Come on," Jeanie said. "Let's feed the chickens."

"Okay." Lily trudged toward the low building surrounded by a high wire fence.

At their approach, chickens ran toward the fence clucking. Lily backed up and handed the pail to Jeanie. "You feed them."

Jeanie snorted. "You baby. There's nothing to be afraid of." She took the pail and edged through the gate.

"Make sure it's closed."

"Big baby. I might as well check for eggs." She ducked into the low building.

"I don't like chickens." Lily shook her head emphatically. "Only baby ones."

"Why is that?"

"Baby chickens is soft and little." Lily's voice grew hard. "Big chickens have these huge claws." She held out her hand with her fingers splayed to show what she meant. "And mean beaks." Wrinkling her nose, she made a snapping motion. "I don't like them." She shuddered.

"Five eggs." Jeanie slipped out the gate and rejoined them.

"Now what?" Lily asked.

"We should take them to Mom," Jeanie said.

"But before that?"

Jeanie rocked back and forth as Lily stubbornly stood with her hands on her hips.

Maryelle watched the exchange with interest, wondering who was the stronger of the two. Finally Jeanie relented. "I guess we could do something else." She set the basket of eggs on the ground. "We'll get them later."

Lily bounced up and down. "What do you want to do?" She directed the question at Maryelle, catching her off guard.

"I don't know what there is to do." She looked toward the barn, where she caught the occasional sound of a man's voice and sporadic hammering. "I know. Let's go see Kingston."

The girls stopped motionless and turned big eyes at her. "We can't go where the men are working," Lily explained. "Dad won't allow it."

Maryelle blinked. She should have known better. It wasn't a safe place for little girls. "I should have thought. How about you tell me what we should do?"

Jeanie continued to stare at her. "Lena's right. You don't know much, do you?"

Stung by the child's words and even more hurt knowing the child overheard things said by her older sister, Maryelle struggled to control her emotions. "I guess maybe I don't know a lot about farms, but I know other things. And what I don't know I can learn."

Jeanie was not about to be deterred. "What other things?"

Suddenly everything Maryelle knew and understood seemed useless in these circumstances.

"Well," Jeanie demanded, "what do you know?"

She began with the first thing that came to mind. "I know I love Kingston very much. That's why I'm here."

"Lena said you stole him."

"Oh. Who did I steal him from? Did he have a girlfriend

waiting for him?" Instantly she regretted asking the child. It was no one's business but Kingston's.

Jeanie shook her head. "Don't think so. But Lena says we lost a lot of our boys."

Maryelle hid a smile at the words coming from the child's mouth, words she was sure Jeanie didn't even understand.

"Why didn't you stay where you belong?"

Maryelle's smile instantly flattened.

three

Ignoring the pain rolling through her, Maryelle answered the child gently. "Because Kingston and I want to be together, and this is his home."

"Come on," Lily demanded. "I want to show you the baby calf. Race ya."

Jeanie took after her sister, with Maryelle following slowly, her heart dragging like something no longer alive. For months, years, she'd ached for the time she and Kingston could be together. Now she discovered she wasn't welcome. At least not by his family. Her dreams had turned into bitter reality.

The girls leaned through the slats of the wooden fence. A reddish cow lifted her head and stared at the intruding humans. A calf, suckling at her side, jerked his head up and scampered away on slender legs. The cow mooed in a calming way and lumbered after her offspring.

"I'm going to call him Scamper," Lily announced. "Isn't that a good name?" She turned to Maryelle for confirmation.

"A most suitable name, I should think." She couldn't stop staring at the wide, soft eyes of the calf, reminding her of a shy deer she'd seen on a trip to the country with her dad.

The calf edged along the fence.

"Here, Calfie, Calfie," Lily crooned until the calf was nose to nose with her. "Maryelle, come and pet him," she whispered.

Maryelle edged forward and gingerly touched the calf's side. "He's soft like a puppy." It was entirely unexpected.

The cow lifted her head high, lowing as she ran toward them. Maryelle jerked back.

Jeanie and Lily laughed. "She can't hurt us," Jeanie said. "The fence is in the way. She only wants to make sure Scamper is all right."

The cow nudged the calf away from the fence.

Maryelle laughed as she looked around. "It's so nice here." She filled her lungs until they were ready to burst. "Everything is so fresh and clean, even the sky." She turned full circle, studying her surroundings—the barn, the trees and bushes, the house with fields spread out behind it. "I can understand why Kingston loves this place and doesn't want to live somewhere else."

Jeanie straightened and fixed her with a curious look. "Where else would he live?"

"No place else. This is his home." She vowed she would make the arrangement work. She'd find a way to break down Lena's coldness and the resentment that oozed from the entire family. No, not everyone, she amended, sensing she'd found acceptance with Kingston's youngest sister. A little voice in her head pointed out that Lena might not be willing to be won over. Maryelle bit her lip. In that case she would learn to ignore Lena.

❧

Kingston stepped back. "Your bath is ready, my lady."

"I didn't mean to put you to so much bother."

It turned out to be a monumental task. After tea—which they called supper—Kingston lifted a copper boiler to the stove and filled it with water. "Maryelle is going to have a bath tonight."

Lena snorted.

Kingston shot her a quelling look. "She's been traveling for days."

While the water heated, he lugged a galvanized tub up the stairs, Maryelle hot on his heels. He paused at the doorway. "There's not much room."

"You could put the one trunk on top of the other. I don't think I'm going to be needing Mom's china or the linens for awhile."

"Good idea." He leaned the tub in the hall and did as she suggested. She spread a linen runner over the top trunk and arranged her photos on it. "My family gallery."

Kingston draped an arm over her shoulder. "One hardly fits." He pointed to Sheba's picture.

"Sheba was always part of the family and a real lady."

"Who mistook herself for royalty if I recall correctly."

"But, of course."

He kissed the tip of her nose. "Welcome home, my brown eyes."

The tension that had mounted to explosion level during the meal eased away in his arms.

"Now about the bath." He brought the tub in the room and carried up hot water.

When she reached to take the pins from her hair, he caught her hands. "Let me." With fingers so gentle they made her want to purr, Kingston pulled out the pins, setting them on the bureau top. Her hair fell down her back.

Kingston raked his fingers through it. "I have dreamed of doing this so many times." He buried his face against her head. "I love your hair."

"I'd like to wash it, but I'd have to sleep with it wet."

"It's early yet. Go ahead. I'll bring up water to rinse it."

She leaned back against him, loathe to break off the contact.

"Your water will be cooling." Kingston stepped away. "I'll be back in a few minutes with fresh water."

Not until he closed the door did she begin unbuttoning her dress.

The tub was too small to stretch out in, but the water felt wonderful. She tipped her head back, reveling in its warmth. The sound of distant laughter reminded her the family was downstairs, and she scrubbed the stains of travel from her skin and stepped from the tub, wrapping herself in a robe before she bent to lather her hair. As if on cue, Kingston arrived in time to rinse it with clean water.

"I'll get rid of this mess." His voice was husky. "Then I'll be right back."

He clattered up and down the steps with buckets. When he'd emptied and dried the tub and opened the door to take it back downstairs, Maryelle caught the sound of tittering giggles.

"You two run along," Kingston ordered.

Maryelle wished she could believe it was Jeanie and Lily in the hall, but she recognized the voices of Lena and Katherine. How long had they been there? What had they heard? Were she and Kingston to be allowed no privacy?

When he returned, he took one look at her face and pulled her down beside him on the bed. "Don't you go worrying about those two. They won't do anything to make me mad at them."

"I thought they'd be glad to see me."

"They will soon love you almost as much as I do. You wait and see."

"I hope you're right."

"Have I ever been wrong?"

She laughed at his confident tone. "Would you admit it if you were?"

"Certainly. Now give me that brush." He gently worked the tangles from her hair, blotting it with a towel as he did. "Too bad we didn't have a fireplace in this room; then I could dry it for you."

"Like back in London." Her voice thickened as she recalled the blissful days of their honeymoon. "Those were the best days of my life."

"Mine too." He kissed her neck. "Just you and me."

"Just you and me," she repeated. "I wish it could be just you and me again."

His hands stilled. "You aren't having regrets, are you?"

Twisting around, she saw his troubled expression and cradled his face in her hands. "Hardly. It will take time as you said. And after being apart all these months, I'm not going to let anything keep me from enjoying you." She would not admit to him she had her doubts about how this arrangement would work out. She would make it work. For Kingston.

His eyes turned solid green.

She leaned forward to plant a kiss on his mouth. Nothing else mattered but the warmth of his arms and the pleasure of his lips.

After some time, he straightened. "Your hair is going to dry all tossed up." He turned her so he could finish brushing it. "Do you want to braid it for the night?"

"If I don't it will look like a bundle of hay; if I do it will be as kinky as old wire." She shrugged.

"I'll braid it." His touch soothed the surface of her feelings like oil on troubled water, at the same time starting a whirlpool of emotion deep within her being.

He finished the braid, securing it with a ribbon before he faced her. "I want you to be happy," he murmured as he bent to kiss her.

"You make me happy," she whispered before his lips touched hers.

As they prepared for bed, Kingston pulled her into his arms. "I wish I could make things easier for you." He kissed the tip of his nose. "But I know God will help us both. I learned to depend on Him during the war. I carried a little book of Psalms in my vest pocket and almost memorized it. In those verses, I discovered He is my shield and my strong defender."

Maryelle snuggled against him, drawing strength from his presence and his words.

"I've thought a lot about when we could be together as man and wife, and one thing I want to do is pray together every night. I don't want us to have any secrets from each other or for either of us to carry burdens alone. Together, with God's help, we can face anything that comes our way." He looked down into her face. "Are you at ease with that?"

"Of course. I've tried it without God and found I didn't like it. You know how I was when you came into my life."

"You thought everyone had abandoned you, even God."

"Remember when you asked if we could go to church together?"

"And you turned those big brown eyes on me and said rather briskly, 'I've rather quit the habit of going to church.'"

Memories warmed her insides. "But you wouldn't hear of not going. You said, 'A man facing the Huns will need more than his wits to survive.' And you literally dragged me there."

He tweaked her nose. "It wasn't that bad. You've got to remember I was facing being deployed to the front lines. I'm not ashamed to admit I was afraid."

At that, she hugged him tight. "I think it was having you admit you needed God that turned me around. I know after you left, I found a great deal of comfort in taking my concerns to Him."

"Let's not lose that dependency and yearning for Him."

"Let's not."

He took her hands and thanked God for her safe arrival and for the joy of being able to return to the farm. "And, God, help us live wisely and patiently and adjust to the new life we now face together. Amen."

"Amen," she whispered.

"Anything you want to add?"

She shook her head, her heart so full she could barely speak. "You've voiced the feelings of my heart." Her soul was satisfied as with the finest of bread and honey. This spiritual maturity was one of the things she appreciated and loved about Kingston. It had drawn her back to the beliefs of her youth that she'd almost abandoned when her parents died. "Have I told you that I love you?"

"Not nearly enough times," he answered before kissing her again.

⤫

She'd vowed to fit in, to ignore Lena's behavior, but it wasn't easy.

She'd watched the girls make bread several times. So when Mother Brown mentioned they would have to make bread today, Maryelle jumped up and pulled out the wide bowl used for that purpose, ignoring the stunned look on Katherine's face.

"What do you think you're doing?" Lena grabbed the bowl from her.

"I can do this." She yanked the dish back.

"You think it's so easy," Lena jeered. "I should let you do it just to prove you wrong, but we can't afford the waste."

"Then what will you let me do?" Maryelle refused to back down.

"Nothing. We don't need you for nothing."

"Well, I'm here. Get used to it. And I need something to do besides trying to be invisible."

Lena suddenly relented. "Very well. You can separate the milk. It's in there." She nodded toward the little pantry where the separator stood.

"Thank you." She'd seen what they did—pour the milk through the clean cloth into the big metal bowl on top, set a big bucket under the bottom chute, a smaller one under the upper chute, and turn the crank. She filled the bowl and grabbed the crank. Nothing. She used two hands, and slowly the handle made a revolution; but nothing came out of the spouts. She pushed harder, and a trickle came out of the upper one, a gush from the bottom. By the time she finished, she was sweating but triumphant, until Father Brown came in and reached for the bottom bucket.

"Who separated the milk?" he yelled.

Maryelle stepped forward. "I did."

Father Brown cast a look at Lena. "Who showed her how to do it?"

Lena smiled. "She said she could do it by herself."

"Next time crank it fast enough to separate the cream." Shaking his head, he took the pail outside.

Maryelle felt her cheeks warming and caught a glimpse of Lena's exultant smile.

After breakfast, ignoring Lena's attempts to push her

aside, she carried dirty dishes to the basin of sudsy water. Katherine was about to plunge her hands into the hot water. "I'll wash if you like," Maryelle offered.

"It's Katherine's job," Lena said. "Why don't you go away? We don't want you here."

Mother Brown stepped from the pantry. "Now, Lena. That's not necessary."

Lena said no more, but her glare was enough to turn Maryelle's heart to stone. She washed the dishes as quickly as she could, then grabbed her coat and headed outside, to where she didn't know or care.

Kingston worked all day. Jeanie went to school. The women were busy refusing every effort Maryelle made to help. Only Lily seemed to have time for her. But this morning even Lily had found something to do on her own.

Maryelle stood in the yard and looked around. Behind the house was a small hill, and she turned toward it, marching past the house until she found a faint path. Her thoughts churned as she walked.

Lena was being entirely unreasonable and downright mean. She had about run out of ideas on how to cope.

She reached a plateau and paused to let her heaving sides settle down. A zephyr of a breeze caught at her hair, and she shook her head. That's when she finally raised her gaze from the ground beneath her feet. The sun glistened on fresh green fields. Spring had come with the promise of renewed life. She filled her lungs with the sweetness of it all, and slowly calm returned.

Toward the edge of the hill was a row of boulders, and she sat on one, looking out over the fields. "It's like an ocean of land," she said softly, never having seen so much open space anywhere else. She folded her hands. One thing she'd learned from Kingston and had found strength in during the war was the value of prayer. "God, my God and guide," she whispered, "help me see how to deal with this situation. Help me do what is right and not act out of hurt feelings. Be my strength and counselor."

"What'cha doin'?"

The unexpected sound of Lily's voice made Maryelle start. "You scared me. Where did you come from?"

The child with eyes and hair so much like Kingston's looked at her as if considering whether or not she should share a secret, then nodded. "I got a hideout here. You want to see it?"

"I'd love to." It warmed her to have this child accept her so easily. If only—she sighed. There was no point in wishing for things to be different.

"Come on," Lily called.

They went down the slope to a thicket of bushes. Lily parted the bushes and crawled inside.

"You're quite sure I can get through there?"

The disembodied voice answered. "It's easy."

"I'm somewhat larger than you." Maryelle was still doubtful.

"Kingston can do it."

That was all the encouragement she needed, and she ducked her head and pushed her way through.

"See—I told you."

They were in a little clearing so sheltered by branches they were invisible from the outside. "This is nice."

Lily waved her arm in a circle. "This is my house." She grabbed Maryelle's hand. "This is where my dollies sleep." Lily pulled back a scrap of old gray blanket to reveal a row of peculiar dolls.

"Did you make these?"

Lily nodded. "My babies."

"They're wonderful." Maryelle bent to examine them. One was a rock with indentations and bumps that gave it the appearance of a face. Lily had fashioned rags and branches to create a body and limbs. Several of the dolls were created from pieces of branches. Another was a shriveled apple. "I love your babies." The dolls were real enough looking to tug at Maryelle's emotions.

Lily nodded and covered her dolls carefully. Maryelle sat cross-legged and let the child study her. Finally Lily said, "I like you." The way she emphasized the word *I*, Maryelle knew she meant in spite of everyone else. She tried not to let it bother her.

"Thank you. I like you too."

"Oh." Lily pressed her hand to her mouth. "I forgot to show you the rest. Come on." She sprang to her feet and led Maryelle to another spot in the clearing. "My kitchen," Lily announced grandly.

"How marvelous." Maryelle was beginning to suspect Lily was a true scrounger. She'd gathered tins, bits of broken dishes, an old bucket, a crate, a broken chair, even what looked like part of a water pump.

"Would you like tea?" Lily regarded her with utmost seriousness.

Maryelle matched her seriousness. "Why, yes, that would be lovely."

Lily pretended to pump water into a large tin, carried it carefully to the upturned crate, and set it to pretend boil. She had salvaged a broken teapot, its spout and half of one side missing.

"Mom says good tea has to be made proper. So I'll do it proper for you." She poured pretend water into the pot and shook it, stared long into its emptiness, poured in some more pretend water, and set the pot on a board between two rocks. She waited almost twenty seconds. "There. That's proper."

Maryelle giggled. "I should say it is."

Lily set out two strange-looking cups—made of curled leaves—and poured tea.

"This is grand," Maryelle said. "Best tea I've ever had."

Lily giggled. "You're funny."

"Hellooo."

Lily sprang to her feet. "It's Kingston. He's come for tea."

Maryelle laughed. "Then do invite him in."

"Okay." She turned toward the opening. "Come for tea, Kingston."

With a grunt and a mumbled complaint about the bushes, Kingston pushed into the clearing. "So this is where you got to." He addressed Maryelle, but it was Lily who answered.

"We're having tea. You want some?"

Smiling at Maryelle over the child's head, he said, "Got any cookies?"

"I got a whole jar of them."

"Then I'll have tea and cookies." He sat at Maryelle's side, his legs folded before him. With two adults and a child in the tiny space, there was little room, but Maryelle suspected Kingston needed no excuse to sit close. "I see you've been invited into the royal chambers." He turned to Lily. "I thought you said this was a secret for you and me."

Lily stared at him, her mouth a little circle. "I forgot."

Kingston ruffled her hair. "I'm only teasing. I don't have any secrets from Maryelle."

The child's glance shifted from one to the other.

"None?"

"Nope."

Her gaze shifted to Maryelle, her eyes asking the same question.

"Nor I from him," Maryelle said. *Unless for his own good.* She had not told him her problems with his family, though she suspected he saw what went on. Sometimes it stung her that he didn't do anything to improve the situation. Instantly she knew she wasn't being fair. What could he do? He loved her. That was enough. Even as she told herself so, she felt a little surge of anger toward Kingston. Which she instantly squelched. It was up to her to make sure this arrangement worked out.

Lily nodded. "It's nice not to have secrets."

"It is, isn't it?" Kingston said. "So when do I get my tea and cookies?"

Lily giggled. "You're silly." She slanted a look at Maryelle. "Isn't he?"

Glad to be pulled back into more pleasant thoughts, Maryelle leaned toward the child. "Sometimes. But you know what?" Lily's eyes grew round. "I like it. Don't you?"

Lily nodded, her expression serious. "I wish he wasn't gone so long."

"Come here, Baby." Kingston pulled her into his arms. "You were just tiny when I left, but every day I thought of you and I prayed for you. I could hardly wait for the day I'd get to see you again." Brother and sister, so alike, cuddled for a bit. "Now you know what?"

Lily shook her head.

"I have to go back to work. And you, little missy, better get back home before Mom sends out a search party."

"Okay."

Kingston ruffled her hair, then planted a kiss on Maryelle's lips. "Bye, you two," he called, as he crawled out.

Lily stared at Maryelle. Then she nodded decisively. "I like him."

"Me too," Maryelle said. "I suppose we should go now."

Lily shrugged. "Guess so."

Maryelle followed the child through the tunnel. They stood side by side looking out over the scene. It seemed Lily was as reluctant as Maryelle to return to reality.

❧

"I've tried," Maryelle told herself several days later. "But nothing seems to work." Lena did everything she could to shut Maryelle out. "I'm bored, bored, bored." So bored, she acknowledged, she had taken to talking to herself. "Enough of this." She stepped from her room and marched down the stairs. Somehow she would find a way to fit into this family. Kingston's family, she reminded herself. He belonged here. He wanted to stay.

four

She paused at the bottom of the stairs, listening to the hum of conversation, and caught a few words, enough to guess they were talking about her. "Proper English miss." "City girl." And the one that stung the most, "Unsuitable." Taking a deep breath, she stepped into the kitchen.

Mother Brown, Lena, and Katherine sat doing handwork.

The conversation died as if it had been shot, and three faces turned toward her. She lifted her chin.

Jeanie was still at school. Maryelle suspected Lily was off playing in her make-believe house. But soon enough the whole family would troop in, and she'd have to face them again. She did not look forward to it. Facing the women was hard enough. The idea of facing the entire family made her stomach twist. But she would not let anyone see how their treatment of her hurt.

"I'll set the table," she announced, ignoring the way they looked at her. "Do we need plates or bowls?"

"Plates," Katherine answered, ducking her head when Lena glowered at her.

"Fine." Maryelle marched to the cupboard and withdrew the stack of plates and set them around the table.

She heard the clatter of boots as the men approached the door. Angus stepped into the house first. Seeing Maryelle laying out the cutlery, his eyes widened before he darted a look at his older sisters.

Maryelle understood he was caught between his sisters and his brother. Determined to ease the situation, she turned her back on Lena's glower and smiled at him. "You've put in a long morning. What have you been doing?"

He shuffled from one foot to the other and mumbled, "Building a new fence."

Kingston entered the kitchen then, his face shining from a recent scrubbing, beads of water clinging to his hairline. "Angus here has grown to a man while I had my back turned." He clapped the boy's shoulder. "He can keep up with me in everything."

Angus darted a look at Kingston. "I been doing your work while you were gone."

"That you have. You have a right to be proud of yourself." Kingston crossed to Maryelle and draped an arm across her shoulders, squeezing her to his side. "And how was your day?"

Maryelle watched the fleeting expression on Angus's face and guessed Angus felt displaced by the return of his older brother. "The usual," she murmured. Wanting to protect Kingston from the hurt of knowing how his sisters treated her and determined to fix the situation on her own, she had done no more than hint at the problems. Suddenly she knew she couldn't keep it from him much longer; she needed his comfort too much. But would he give it? Was it possible he would choose his family over their marriage? It was why she held back from telling him. Besides, she had one more plan to try.

She waited until they had gone to their room for the night, glad that darkness came shortly after supper so they could spend some private time together.

It was too early to go to bed, so they sat together on the floor. Maryelle loved this time away from the darting glances of the rest of the family—she and Kingston alone together. He sprawled across the floor, his head at her knees, running his finger up and down her arm.

"What did you do today?" she asked

"We almost finished the fence. Tomorrow we'll complete the job and put the cows out there."

"I know so little about what you do, how the farm works." She paused. "Could I go with you tomorrow and see what you do?" She had wanted to go with him from the first but felt shy around Father Brown and Angus. And no invitation had been issued.

Kingston's finger halted. His expression flattened. "I don't think that would be a good idea."

"Why ever not? I thought it was a good idea."

Kingston flopped to his back, his hands under his head. "Trust me—it's not."

She waited, but he didn't seem inclined to explain himself.

"Is there some reason?"

His eyes were neither blue nor green, but a strange stormy color. "I suppose there must be or I wouldn't have said it."

He offered no more.

"Are you going to tell me the reason, or is it a secret?"

He jerked his head to indicate his uncertainty.

"Now I'm really curious. Remember we promised no secrets." She pushed back the nagging accusation of her own withheld information.

"Come on, Kingston. Tell me what you're hiding." She tickled his ribs. He jerked away, capturing her hands.

"It's not a big deal, I guess. It's just that Dad doesn't like women folk around outside. He figures a woman's place is in the house."

Maryelle drew back and pulled in her chin. "Where has he been the last four years? Doesn't he know that it was women who kept the country running while the men went off to the trenches? Why, I ran my father's business single-handedly. I even went on the annual spring buying trip on my own after he was killed." She glowered at Kingston.

"Hey, wait. Don't be mad at me. I just told you how my dad felt. Not how I feel." He pulled her down on his chest. She remained stiff. "Don't you think I'd keep you by my side day and night if I had a choice?" He chuckled. The sound rumbling in her ear broke down her defenses, and she smiled against his chest. "Course I probably wouldn't get a lot of work done, would I?" He hugged her tight.

She let her breath out in a whoosh. "It seems you work all day long. I barely get to see you except at mealtimes, and then everyone else is there."

"There's always a lot of work to be done on a farm. You should have seen that already. Even the women have an endless round of work to do."

"Then you'd think they'd let me help." She hadn't meant to tell him.

"What do you mean?"

She sat up so she could see him. "I didn't mean to say anything. I don't want to hurt you."

His eyes darkened. "No secrets, remember?"

She nodded. "I've been aching to tell you anyway." She took a deep breath. "I want to help. I want to learn how to do everything." She tried to smile and failed. "But it seems they don't want my help." A shudder raced across her shoulders. Her eyes flooded with tears.

Kingston jerked up and pulled her into his arms. "I didn't know. I've seen Lena looking nasty, but I didn't know what she was doing." He tipped her head back and wiped the tears from the corner of her eyes. "Lena is bitter because the boy she cared about didn't come back from the war."

"I'm sorry," she whispered.

"I am too, but that doesn't excuse her behavior. She has no right to resent you for it." He gazed across the room. "I'm guessing Katherine follows her lead, and Mom turns her back and ignores what's going on."

Maryelle nodded. "I've tried. I do what I can without Lena jumping in and telling me they don't need my help. About all I've been allowed to do is one of the little girls' jobs." Until now, saying it aloud, she hadn't admitted even to herself how it hurt to be treated as an incompetent child. "I've worked all my life. I was knee-high to a grasshopper when Dad showed me how to sort and display potatoes and carrots. By the time I was school age, I could unpack crates and fill the bins as well as he. I was only sixteen when he went off to France, leaving me to run the business with Mom's help. Two weeks later he was dead." Her voice dropped to a whisper. "And when Mom quit living, I managed to care for her and run the business without any help." She flung her hands out in defeat. "Now here I am. Treated like a child." She gulped hard.

Kingston pulled her into his arms, crooning, "My poor Maryelle. What are we going to do?" He rocked her until her breathing grew steady, then tipped her chin up. "What do you want to do about it?"

She wanted to say, *What can I do? Everything I try fails.* Besides, all she wanted was reassurance of Kingston's love. And to have him to herself. But she couldn't bring herself to say so. What if he told her he never intended to leave the farm? Not even for her? So she gave a little shrug. "What do you mean?"

She watched him struggle with his answer. "I suppose if you really want to we could find someplace else to live."

She didn't know whether to laugh or cry. "Thank you, Kingston, my love, but where would we go? What would you do? You said yourself that all you know and care about is farming." She refrained from adding "this farm." She was certain it mattered more than she did, but she would not resort to self-pitying remarks.

"I'm sure we could find something."

She smiled. He sounded as uncertain as she felt.

"I would like to have things work out," she said, hoping to drive away the confusion in his expression. "But I'm not sure what more I can do."

"I will speak to Lena."

"Won't that make things worse?"

"I hope not. Lena hasn't always been like this." He snorted. "Not that she's been easy to live with. But let me give it a try." He gripped her shoulders. "But I want you to promise you'll tell me if things get worse." He crushed her to his chest. "I want you to be happy."

"And I want you to be happy." She understood that his happiness was wrapped up in the farm he loved. "I will find a way of making peace with the others." The vow was as much for her as for him. "Somehow things will work out."

"We will pray about it."

Maryelle closed her eyes as Kingston prayed aloud for a solution to their problem.

❧

When she woke the next morning, Kingston's side of the bed was empty. Why was he up so early on a Sunday, the only day there was any rest around the farm? She scrambled from the bed and donned her Sunday clothes. Must have been something mighty important to take him from her side so early.

Downstairs she found Kingston packing sandwiches in a tin and explaining to his mother, "Maryelle and I are going for a picnic after church." He flashed Maryelle a look full of promise.

She couldn't contain her smile. An afternoon alone with Kingston. The thought of it made breakfast pass quickly.

As soon as they finished the meal, she followed him outside, where he had the buggy waiting. Since the first Sunday, they had gone to church in the buggy while the others crowded into the car that was Father Brown's pride and joy.

"It's not much better than a tin Lizzie," he'd said that first Sunday.

"What's a tin Lizzie?" Lily had asked.

"That's what we called the tin hats we had in the war. We used them to carry water in. We even washed in them." He shook his head. "I won't be riding in anything that reminds me of one."

And so Maryelle and Kingston had gone in the buggy while the rest rode proudly in the motor vehicle, a fact that Maryelle envied them not at all. She much preferred having Kingston to herself. And this Sunday she would have him to herself in the afternoon too. She hugged the thought to her.

Maryelle had discovered the kindly old minister to be full of the wisdom of God. Every Sunday she came away refreshed and encouraged for the week ahead, and today was no exception, even though her anticipation of the afternoon made it difficult to sit still.

"Where are we going?" she asked as soon as they drove away from the church.

"I've neglected to show you this beautiful country. Today I will begin to make up for my failing."

He sounded so serious, she hugged his arm. "You have no failings, my dear Kingston."

He laughed and pulled her into the hollow under his arm. "I'll see that you are rewarded for that, sweet brown eyes."

"What wonderful thing are you showing me today?" Not that it really mattered. Having the day together was wonder enough. For one whole afternoon she would push aside the way her insides had grown tighter and tighter, like a knot pulled from both ends, at the way his family shut her out.

"The river," he answered.

"The river?"

"It's one of the prettiest sights around. Hope there aren't too many others with the same idea."

"Me too," she whispered.

"It is beautiful," she agreed a short time later when he pulled under the trees.

"I'll show you around after we eat." He jumped down and helped her, then reached for the box containing the lunch. He spread a blanket under the pine trees. "Come on, Mrs. Brown—let's eat." He took her hand and prayed for the meal, then handed her a sandwich. "Built with my own hands," he bragged.

She took a bite. "Um. No wonder it tastes so good."

"Oh, that special taste is because I forgot to wash." He laughed as she wrinkled her nose.

She took a couple more bites, then stared at him wide-eyed, gulped hard, and let her mouth drop open.

"What? What's the matter?" he demanded.

"I can't believe you did that."

"Did what?"

"Ate that horrible big bug without even slowing down. Was he tasty?"

Kingston spat, practically dropping the rest of his sandwich. "Why didn't you say something?"

"I did."

He cast her an annoyed look. "I mean before I ate it."

She shrugged, keeping an indifferent expression on her face. "I figured anyone who would make sandwiches without washing wouldn't mind a bug or two."

He gaped at her as he grasped the idea that she had tricked him. "Why, you dirty rotten stinker." And he lunged for her.

She knew what to expect and jumped out of his reach. "Tsk, tsk. No need to resort to name calling."

He rose to his feet, growling. "Count yourself lucky that so far name calling is all you've experienced."

He grabbed for her. She danced away and, shrieking, ran headlong through the trees.

He crashed after her.

She knew she couldn't hope to outrun him; her only hope of escape was to find someplace to hide. She skidded around the next tree, saw some bushes, and veered to the right. The ground dropped away without warning. She lost her footing and stumbled behind a thicket, landing in a heap.

With a loud roar, Kingston barreled down the slope after her, landing on his feet at her side. He threw himself to the ground beside her and wrapped his arms around her. "Now I've got you," he jeered.

"Right where I want you." She laughed.

"You're a tease," he said.

"You like it."

She wanted to continue teasing, but his face was so close, his breath hot on her cheek, his eyes so green, his hair falling over his forehead and catching the sunshine in flames of red. Her eyes rested on his lips. He lowered his head until their lips met in a warm, gentle touch.

He pulled back. "Seems I've waited a long time to have you all to myself."

She turned on her side so she could study him. "Too long. But you're certainly worth waiting for."

"You think so? Then you aren't having any regrets about marrying me?"

She trailed a finger down his nose and across his lips.

He captured her hand and pressed it to his heart.

"Not a one," she whispered. "Not a one." Her only regret was she couldn't have him to herself every day, but there wasn't any point in ruining the day by thinking about it.

He drew her close. She rested her forearms on his chest and smiled down on him.

"You're right. I like everything about you from your lovely dark hair to your warm brown eyes to your sweet little mouth."

Her cheeks grew warm. "Now who's crazy?"

He chuckled. "Yes, but you like it." He scrambled to his feet, pulling her up. "Come on—let's go for a walk by the river."

They walked along the bank of the river on a narrow path.

"It's lovely here," Maryelle said. "And so peaceful. I love the sound of the water rippling over the rocks."

"Do you hear a squirrel scolding us?"

"And crows too." They walked on. Maryelle strained to catch the sound of many different birds. "I've noticed one thing about this country."

"What's that?"

"It smells so good. At the farm I can smell the trees and flowers."

"And the barns?"

"When the wind is right, I do. But I'm used to petrol and dust and garbage bins." She filled her lungs. "Smell the pines."

He pulled her to his side. "I'm glad you like it."

"I do like this country."

"How do you feel about the farm?" His voice was calm, but she knew it was a question with special importance. She carefully considered her words.

"What I've seen of it, I find fascinating. I love the new calves and baby pigs. I love being able to go outside and see the fields." She hugged his arm. "I love living on a farm."

She felt his tension ease.

He found a fallen tree and pulled her down beside him to sit on it. "You sure you don't miss London?"

She considered his question. "I miss my home, but it's no longer my home. The couple who bought the shop could hardly wait for me to leave so they could start changing things." She shrugged. "Things are different here, but it's all I have." The truth of her words sent an ache into her heart. Even if she wasn't determined to make this situation work for Kingston's sake, she didn't have any other alternative. This was all she had.

"I've been thinking about what you told me last night. I confess it's bothered me. But I haven't been able to come up with anything I think will help."

"I've been thinking too."

"Did you come up with something?"

"Maybe. You know how I told you every year Dad took me with him to visit the different market gardens and purchase produce for the season?"

He nodded.

"I loved walking through the gardens and seeing how different people did different things. I always wanted to try my hand at growing a garden. Kingston, is there some reason I couldn't have a garden? It would give me something useful to do."

"But Mom already grows a big garden."

"I know. I thought we could sell or give away the extra produce." Her shoulders slumped. "I guess it doesn't make much sense."

"I don't see why not. I'll help you myself."

She flew into his arms. "Thank you."

He squeezed her tight. "It's nothing."

She put her head against his shoulder. "Is it any wonder I love you so much?"

"Come on, brown eyes—let's see some more of the river."

"Umm." She didn't move. "If we don't, I suppose I'll never hear the end of it."

Laughing, he pulled her to her feet. "And you'll regret it the rest of your life."

"That I doubt, but come on."

They continued until they came to a grassy spot. "Want to rest?"

"I'm not—" She hesitated. What did it matter if she was tired or not? The thought of cuddling in his arms was reason enough to stop.

They found a broad tree to lean on. Kingston waited until she eased herself to the ground and got her back comfortable on the trunk before he dropped to her side, squirming around to lay his head in her lap.

"This is the life," he said softly. "You and me forever."

She spread her fingers through his hair, liking the feel of it between her fingers. He reached up one hand and cupped her head. "I can't imagine life getting any better than this."

She nodded, ignoring the warning voice in her mind that reminded her things had not changed at home.

He must have read her mind for he hugged her. "I'm sure things will get better. If I wasn't, I wouldn't ask you to bear with it."

She nodded. "It will just take time."

"That's right." He brushed her nose with the back of his finger. "Why are we wasting our time talking about it when we could be doing this?" He pulled her down and kissed her.

❧

The next evening he announced after supper, "Maryelle and I are going to plant a garden."

Maryelle felt the stunned silence to the soles of her feet.

Father Brown harrumphed. "The garden is Mom's doing."

"This will be ours." Kingston folded his arms and waited. "I figure that spot past the trees would work up real nice. I'll plow it this evening."

"Sounds like a waste of time to me," Lena said.

"I have nothing else to do." Maryelle was determined to remain firm.

"Sure, and why not let her do it?" Father Brown made it sound as if it were somehow a great sacrifice.

Lena darted a look at Katherine, then said half under her breath, "Probably won't grow anyway."

Angus watched the reaction of the others, reveling, Maryelle thought, in their disapproval.

Only Lily approved. "Will you grow flowers? Mom never does."

Maryelle smiled. "I hadn't decided, but it sounds good. Maybe you can help me select which ones to plant."

She fairly bounced in her chair. "Goody goody gumcakes."

"Planted much before, have you?" It was Father Brown, and she was not deceived by his innocent question. They all hoped she'd fail, but she would not. It would be the best garden any of them had ever seen.

"No, but I know vegetables, and I like to see them growing."

"Sometimes they don't grow as we hope." It was the first thing Mother Brown had said on the subject, and Maryelle guessed it would probably be the last. Mother Brown seemed to have developed an incredible ability to ignore the world around her and retreat into her thoughts.

"I guess we'll learn as we go." Kingston pushed himself away from the table. "You coming?" he asked Maryelle.

She needed no second invitation and hurried after him.

He took her past the trees to a weed-overgrown bit of land. "Dad plowed this one year, then decided it was too small to bother with. It will need some work, but what do you think?"

"It's wonderful. As to work, I welcome the prospect."

"Then I'll get started on it right now."

While he was away getting the plow, she walked the length and breadth of it, pausing to kick a lump of dirt, noting the green carpet of weeds already well on their way to producing another crop. And then Kingston returned with the horse and plow. "You stand back there and watch how it's done."

Grinning at the way he preened before her, she plunked down on a grassy spot and watched him lay over neat rows of black earth. The musky smell pulled at her senses. She scooped up a handful of freshly turned soil, squeezing her fist around it, smelling it before she crumbled it and tossed it down.

Kingston paused as he drew to her side.

She scooped up another handful and threw it in the air. "If only my dad could see me now."

Kingston grinned at her. "I'm sure he'd wonder what you were doing."

"No, he knew I loved to see things grow." Her thoughts raced backward. "I used to ask so many questions of everyone that I wonder why he didn't get fed up with me. But all he did was smile and nod his head. It was as if he knew I had to know." A gentle smile tugged her lips. "I miss him."

Kingston reached out and touched the tip of her nose. "I guess you do."

"They're fond memories though."

He nodded and returned to his task, finishing it in a short time. As he took the horse back, she tramped across the now-plowed garden spot. Already she could see she would have her work cut out for her even before she could plant.

When Kingston returned, she was yanking grass roots from the sod. "Here—try this." He handed her a hoe. "Most of it is weeds. They'll be dead by morning. It's the grass you'll have to work on."

"I am." She grunted as she hacked away at a resistant clod.

They worked side by side until it was too dark to see.

"Oh, my aching back," she moaned as she straightened.

"If you want work, you've got work."

"I love the smell of the soil and the feel of it on my hands."

"You'd best be getting some gloves, or your hands will soon be as rough as a board."

They stood side by side. "I can hardly wait until morning so I can finish here."

He kissed her nose. "Don't figure on doing it in one day."

❧

Ignoring her aching muscles, she rushed through breakfast the next morning, gathering the dishes and plunging them into hot water with never a mind about the sharp looks cast in her direction. She washed them up and then headed for the garden.

Before Kingston left, he'd handed her a broad-brimmed hat and a pair of gloves. "I don't suppose there's any point in telling you to take it easy, but at least protect your face and hands."

She thought they had done a large share last night, but in the light she saw how many chunks of sod needed to be broken up and lumps of weeds to thrash out—a lot of work. But as she knelt in the dirt, she breathed deeply and thanked God for the opportunity.

Kingston wandered over later in the morning to announce, "It's time for dinner."

She sat back and moaned, grabbing her neck.

He reached out and pulled her to her feet. "I told you not to overdo it." He massaged her neck.

"I'll be fine," she murmured, stifling another moan as she straightened. "I'll get used to it."

It took her three days of steady work with Kingston helping in the evenings before she felt as if the ground was ready. On the fourth day she wandered the perimeter. She had removed every stone she could find, piling them at one end. She had tidied the edges with a spade. Sighing, she leaned on a hoe. In her eagerness, she had worked herself out of a job.

"What'cha thinking?" Kingston's voice almost in her ear made her jump in surprise.

"Where did you come from?"

"Scared you, huh?"

She waved the hoe at him. "You're lucky I have nerves of steel, or I might have swung this at you and cracked your head."

"Then I wouldn't be able to offer you a ride to town."

"Really? I can go to town with you? Can I get seeds there?"

"'Spect so." He narrowed his eyes. "Maybe you should wash your face first. I'll wait for you in front of the barn."

"I'll be there in a jiffy." She raced for the house and burst through the door, ignoring the startled looks on Katherine's and Lena's faces. Mother Brown was absent, perhaps working in her own garden or having a rest.

"Face is dirty," Lena said.

Maryelle nodded. "Kingston already told me. That's why I'm here. I've got to wash so I can go to town with him."

"Why should you get to go to town?" Lena's face grew dark.

"Because he asked me."

"I haven't been except on Sunday for ages," Katherine said.

Maryelle hesitated. Although she ached for a chance to be alone with Kingston, she knew Katherine had offered her a chance to make a friend of the girl. "I'm sure you could come along if you like."

Katherine half rose, then caught Lena's sharp look and sank back down, ducking her head. "I don't want to," she muttered.

"Another time, perhaps." Maryelle hurriedly washed her face and dashed back out, having no desire to run broadside into Lena's tongue.

five

In town, Kingston pulled up before a hardware store. "Do you want me to come with you to get the seeds?"

"No, I can do it. Just aim me in the right direction."

He pointed across the street, then handed her some bills. "If you need any more just tell Mr. Scott I'll settle up before we leave."

She looked at the still unfamiliar bills. "How long do I have?"

"I have to see about repairs for the disk. I expect to be awhile, so take your time. It's a small town. I'll find you when I want you."

"Thank you, Kingston."

He waved as she hurried across the street. She knew what she wanted—root vegetables, salad greens, and flowers. In the store she found the seeds as well as a pleasant shopkeeper who helped her make her selection. "These do well here," he said, tilting a package of carrot seeds toward her. "They're a good keeper too."

"Keeper?"

"You know. In the root cellar."

"Ah, yes." She added it to her growing pile. "Now what about flowers?"

Again he showed her a selection, and she chose most of them.

"Anything else?"

She nodded. "Gloves."

"I have just the thing for you." He brought out a pair for her to try.

"Perfect," she said and paid for everything. "Thank you for your help."

"Thank you for your business, and welcome to the community. I hope you're finding it to your liking."

"Actually I've seen very little of the town. Kingston drove me through it the first day, but I can't say I noticed much. Then we've come to church on Sunday." The church was situated before the rest of the buildings, so she'd had little opportunity to see anything more.

"Then you haven't had a chance to see all the good things here. We have thirty thriving businesses: pharmacy, dry goods, hardware, blacksmith, a lawyer. The doctor has his office over there. We have three churches and a good school." He had come to stand by her side and pointed out the window. "Even a nice library—"

"A library? Where?"

"Right around that corner and past the alley."

Maryelle peered through the window. The wagon stood across the street, but she saw no sign of Kingston. "If Kingston comes looking for me, will you tell him I've gone to the library?"

"Certainly. Glad to be of help."

She hurried in the direction the shopkeeper had indicated and soon found the narrow white building with a sign assuring her she'd found the right place. A smaller sign informed her the library was open Thursday, Friday, and Saturday. Grateful she'd happened on a day when it was open, she stepped inside. She waited for her eyes to adjust to the dimness and filled her lungs with the smell of books and oiled floors.

A few minutes later, she emerged with two publications on growing a garden in Alberta and two novels that would help pass the time once she got the seeds in the ground.

That evening Kingston helped her stake out the rows and plant the seeds.

"This was a good idea of mine," he said, covering the pea seeds with the damp soil.

"What idea was that?" She marched ahead of him, dropping seeds a few inches apart.

"The garden, of course. Wasn't it a good idea?"

She laughed, pausing long enough to meet his blue-green gaze. "Guess this is one of those times when you and I are one, but you're the one."

He laughed. "Yup."

"You know something? I don't care whose idea it is; all I care is I finally have something productive to do. Something I've always wanted to do."

"I'll make a real little farmer of you yet."

She grinned. "I don't think you'd have to work very hard at it." Again she dropped peas into the narrow trench Kingston had prepared. "Despite what Lena seems to think about my being a city girl, I'm really just a working class girl with a yen to get my hands dirty."

He rested the hoe against his leg and grabbed her hand. "I think your dreams have been fulfilled."

She laughed at the way he shook his head over her dirt-soiled, roughened hands.

"Whatever happened to my fine English miss?"

She finished the row and waited for him to catch up. "I think she's turning into a farmer."

He dropped the hoe at the end of the row and checked over

his shoulder both ways before he grabbed her in a bear hug. She clung to him. "Mrs. Brown, you have dirt on your nose." He kissed the spot, then lowered his lips to her mouth.

He released her and turned so they looked at the neatly planted rows. "Your garden is all planted, Mrs. Brown. What are you going to do now?"

She shrugged. "Guess I'll have to wait."

ﾞﾞ

It was harder to wait than she could have imagined. The next morning she did up the few chores she was allowed to help with and wandered down to her garden, a book and her Bible in her hand. She found a grassy spot and spent a few minutes reading the Bible and praying for God's strength to be patient and loving in this family. *Especially, God, help me to trust Kingston's love.* Feeling she had to compete with the farm and his family for Kingston's affections made her ache inside. When Kingston wasn't at her side, she felt so alone, as abandoned as she'd felt when her parents died. He had helped her find her way back to God at that time. She vowed she'd not lose her faith again. She would trust God to lead her through this trying time to something better.

Feeling new strength and encouragement, she began to read the garden manual she'd borrowed from the library.

Later Lily wandered by to visit. "You want to see some baby kittens?"

Glad of the diversion, glad of any diversion, and equally eager to see some baby kittens, she jumped up. "I'd love to see some baby kittens."

Lily bounced toward the barn. "Mitten had them in the loft." She glanced over her shoulder. "You think you can climb the ladder?"

Maryelle grinned to think that she appeared so old to this child. "You think you can help me if I can't?"

Lily drew to a halt. "I don't think so. I'm just a little girl."

Maryelle laughed. "Don't fret. I'll be fine."

"Good." Lily led the way into the shadowed interior of the barn. Maryelle had not been there before, although she'd wanted to see it. Somehow she had the feeling that unless she was invited, she wouldn't be welcome.

Shafts of light slanted through the high narrow windows, beaming their fingers on the dust Lily's restless feet kicked up as she waited. Stalls lined each side of the barn; an array of reins, yokes, and other things she recognized as being used with the horses hung from nails. Maryelle breathed in a potpourri of scents—dusty hay, old horse sweat, worn leather, fresh dung; smells both familiar and strange, neither pleasant nor unpleasant, and yet exciting.

"Up here," Lily called, hanging from a rung of a ladder nailed to the wall.

Maryelle climbed after her through a square hole in the ceiling to the loft, the floor smooth and slippery with bits of hay. She followed the child to a corner and saw the cat she'd met before, surrounded by five tiny little bodies. "They're so small," she whispered.

Lily sat cross-legged, petting the mother cat. "You can touch them if you want."

Maryelle scooted close and reached toward a mottled kitten.

The mother cat, purring contentedly under Lily's petting, suddenly lifted her head and made an inquiring noise.

Maryelle jerked back. "She doesn't mind, does she?"

"It's okay, Mitten," Lily crooned. "She won't hurt them."

The cat continued to keep her eyes on Maryelle as she

lifted one tiny body in her cupped hands. "I've never seen anything so small except a mouse." Sheba had been scampering about, bright-eyed and full of mischief, when Dad brought her home. These little bodies were helpless, their eyes still closed.

She put the kitten back. It nuzzled until it found a place to nurse.

"You like cats?" Lily asked.

"Umm. They're my favorite." She missed Sheba so much.

"What was your cat's name?"

"Sheba. Queen of the cats."

Lily giggled. "What happened to her?"

"She died of old age."

"Did you cry?"

Tears flooded her eyes at the memory. "Yes, I cried a great deal."

"Oh." Lily seemed at a loss for words at the idea of an adult crying.

Maryelle smiled. "But Kingston was there, and he made me feel better."

"Good."

"In fact, it was Kingston who thought she should have a proper burial."

Lily turned to look at Maryelle, her wide eyes dark green in the dim light, her mouth a little circle. "What did you do?"

Maryelle shifted to a more comfortable position, glad to talk to someone she was sure would share her sense of loss over her cat. "I guess I'll have to tell you the whole story."

Lily nodded vigorously.

"Sheba was very old. About all she did was climb down off

my bed long enough to get something to eat and then go back and sleep some more. Kingston said she was a lazy cat, but of course he was teasing. I'm just so glad he was there when she died because I was very sad."

Lily nodded her understanding. "I would cry if Mitten died."

"I told him I couldn't bear the thought of getting rid of her body, and he said, 'Why don't we take the bus out to the country and bury her under a tree somewhere?' So that's what we did." Sheba had been the last living thing holding her to London. When the time came, Maryelle found it rather easy to sell the shop. She was completely free to join Kingston. She had no other place she wanted to be. She sighed. If only she felt as if she belonged here.

"I wish I could have a cat in the house," Lily said. "I'd let her sleep with me every night."

Maryelle petted the five tiny kittens. "It's nice. Sheba was my best friend." They'd played together when they were both young. And Maryelle had found comfort in her soft fur and rough tongue when her parents had died. "I still miss her."

To Maryelle's surprise, Lily scrambled over and gave her a hug. She held the child close and was comforted.

❧

Maryelle sprawled under the shade of the tree on her well-worn grassy spot. She'd read all her library books, including the gardening guides, several times. She'd dusted and rearranged the items in her bedroom repeatedly. She'd practically begged to be allowed to bake something, do anything, but Mother Brown had gone to her room, and Lena had refused Maryelle's help in her usual blunt way.

She rolled over on her back and stared at the leaves

dancing against the blue sky. The plants were only beginning to poke their tiny leaves through the soil, but she'd
weeded so diligently there wasn't a weed or a blade of grass
in the garden. She tried to read some more in her Bible
and for awhile found it diverting and encouraging. She
prayed for God to send something interesting into her life.
But nothing happened, except the leaves whispered.

She had nothing in the whole world to do. She was bored,
bored, bored.

She sat up, pulling her knees to her chest. The chickens
scratched and clucked inside their fence. Behind them from
the pigpen rose sounds of grunting contentment and a rather
unpleasant odor. A few cows were visible in the field behind
the barn.

But Maryelle saw no sign of anyone human. Where was
Lily? The child would have provided some welcome diversion.

But she hadn't seen Lily since lunch. Perhaps she had gone
to her hideout up the hill. Maryelle considered trying to find
the child, but it wasn't childish company she longed for; she
wanted something useful to do.

If only she and Kingston had their own home, she could
be busy cooking and cleaning and washing.

She leaned her head against her knees. How long before
they could be on their own? She straightened. Kingston had
never come right out and said what he planned—only that
there wasn't enough money to build something for them and
nothing around they could live in. If she knew how long she
must endure this arrangement, perhaps she could be patient.

With the light lasting longer in the evenings, she saw less
and less of Kingston, and it grew increasingly difficult to be
patient. The ache inside her grew. All she wanted was to be

allowed to love her husband and not have to share him with so many other demands. Not that she thought having a home of their own would mean he danced at her side all day long. She wouldn't want that. *Please, God, I want to feel like a wife. I want to know he loves me as much as the farm.*

At that moment, Kingston stepped from the barn, paused to check the length of leather in his hands, then ducked around the corner.

"No better time than the present to find out what's ahead," she murmured and jumped up, dusting her skirt before she followed in his direction.

It took several minutes to reach the barn. She rounded the corner and saw Kingston facing his father.

Having no desire to discuss anything in front of Father Brown, Maryelle halted in the shadow of the barn, hoping the men would part and go their separate ways. Instead Father Brown stepped toward Kingston.

"You ain't got the brains God gave a sack of hammers." Father Brown's voice was low and guttural. She thought he must be joking, but she heard no humor in his tone.

"It was already cracked," Kingston replied, his voice low and calm. "Bound to give way sooner or later."

Father Brown stood beside a piece of farm machinery, a spanner in his hand. "Don't give me that. You always did have a knack for busting everything you touched."

Kingston didn't move.

"Bet you that high and mighty little English girl ain't even happy to be here with you."

Her dear husband didn't reply, but she bled for him. How often did he endure these degrading remarks?

Father Brown shook the spanner in his face. "Got nothing

to say to that, do ya? Too close to the truth, maybe." He snorted. "She'll get tired of you soon enough. Fact is, I can't figure out why she's still here. I expected her to pack it in and head back home long ago."

Maryelle took one step forward, an angry protest on her lips. How dare he say things like that to Kingston—the finest man she'd ever met? She would never leave him and go back to England. What was there to go back for? Her heart and soul were here with her husband.

"I think we can fix it up in a jiffy." Kingston turned toward the broken machine.

His father blocked his move. " 'We'? I like the way you say 'we.' You break 'em. I fix 'em. So where does 'we' come into it?"

Kingston faced his father. He spoke not a word.

"You never was worth a hill of beans."

Maryelle reached toward her dear, sweet husband, wanting to stop this attack. She wanted to say his father was wrong—Kingston was worth ten of anyone else in this cruel family—but she didn't know if speaking would make things worse. She remained in the shadows, her mouth parched, her heart heavy, her arms aching to hold her husband.

"The army didn't seem to agree with you." Kingston's voice was still calm. "They thought I was good enough to lead a troop against the Huns."

"Too bad you didn't get shot out there. Would have saved me a bunch of trouble."

Maryelle thought her heart would rip from its place.

Kingston only shrugged. "Well, I'm here. And I'm ready to work. Just as soon as we repair this." He bent toward the machine.

Father Brown roared. "Get your hands off it before you

bust it for good." He raised the spanner above his head and swung at Kingston.

Maryelle grabbed for the barn as her legs weakened beneath her.

"I'll kill you. I swear I will."

Kingston ducked away. The spanner missed him by a fraction of an inch. He jumped back, his arms at his side. Maryelle saw the ready tension in his body. "If you kill me, who will do your work?" His voice revealed no emotion.

"I managed while you was gone, didn't I?" He breathed so hard Maryelle could hear him from where she stood. "Me and Angus, we managed."

"The fences were broken down, the loft floor damaged, and several fields weed infested—but, yes, you managed." Kingston dropped the hunk of iron he held. "Maybe you'll manage again." He turned on his heel and strode away toward the barn. He glanced up, and Maryelle felt his gaze bore right through her.

"You get back here." Father Brown threw the spanner. It caught Kingston in the shoulder, but Kingston marched on without slowing or turning. His father roared a string of curses.

Maryelle could face no more. She sped away before Father Brown saw her, her heart beating in her ears like a marching drum. She ran past the house, past her garden, her lungs begging for air. She didn't slow down until she crested the hill behind the house, where she collapsed in a heaving, sobbing heap on the ground.

Arms enclosed her. "You shouldn't have been there."

She hadn't heard Kingston following her, but she readily turned into his embrace. "How could he do that?" she sobbed. "He tried to kill you."

He sat down and pulled her into his arms. "He would never kill me." He gave a snorting laugh. "Who would do his work if he did?"

She clung to him. "It was awful. The things he said to you." She drew a shuddering breath. "How could you stand it?"

He shrugged. "I don't let it bother me."

She tipped her head up so she could see his face. "But it does bother you. I can tell by your voice. And your eyes."

He looked deep into her eyes, and she saw just how much it hurt him. His pain was her pain, and she groaned. He pulled her tight, burying his face in her neck. They clung to each other. It was several minutes before she could speak. "How long has this been going on?"

He sighed a sigh that seemed to come from deep inside him. "All my life."

His words shivered through her body.

"I used to think maybe I wasn't his son. Asked Mom about it once, and all she said was, have a look at your grandfather. She meant Dad's father. And she was right. I look so much like him it's uncanny." He shrugged again. "I don't know why he treats me as he does. It's only me."

Maryelle held her tongue. From what she'd seen, the rest of the family did one of two things: Do as Lena had and develop a tongue that would stop even Father Brown. Jeanie was well on the way to developing the same sharpness. Or retreat into sullen pliability as had Angus and Mother Brown. Katherine, she wasn't sure of. Lily alone, besides Kingston, remained free spirited despite the family dynamics. Suddenly she feared for little Lily as she grew older.

"Why do you put up with it? Wouldn't it be better to leave?"

"I did leave, remember? I went to war. And discovered I missed the farm so much it didn't matter what my father said. When I came back, I found the place falling into rack and ruin. It tore my heart to see how it had been neglected. In the few months since I've been home, it's finally beginning to look decent again."

"I know how much you love this place. It's all you ever talked about when we were courting, as I recall."

He gave a short laugh. "I thought you liked it."

"I did." She lay silent against him, thinking of the things he had said—how much he cared about this place—but Father Brown's vicious words, his physical threats, blotted out everything else. "How do you stand it?" she whispered.

six

"By the time I get back, he will have forgotten all about it. We'll just get on with the work as if it never happened." Kingston paused. "Until next time."

Maryelle's teeth chattered. "He could have killed you."

"I doubt it. Besides, I'd never let him."

His words did nothing to calm her fears. What if his father one day flew into a rage when Kingston wasn't watching? She breathed deeply to calm the nausea sweeping through her.

"We need a place of our own." A retreat for both of them.

"And we'll get it. Eventually."

She pressed on. "How long is eventually?"

"I can't say. Father thinks I've spent far too much of his money repairing things. He doesn't pay me a regular wage, so it's hard to save anything." His face was troubled. "I'm not much comfort, am I?"

She stroked his face. "I'm not trying to increase your troubles; it's just that we need to establish our own home."

"I want it as much as you."

She doubted that to the depths of her soul. "Would you be able to ask your father for a loan to build a small house?"

"I don't think he'd like it."

A shiver of fear raced through her at what those words had suddenly come to signify. "Then, by all means, don't ask him. Something will work out."

"I wish I could see what."

"Listen—if you can stand it, I can stand it. In fact"—she placed her hand on his chest—"as long as we stand together, we'll be fine." Somehow she'd find a way to survive.

He hugged her tight and kissed her nose. "Have I told you how much I love you?"

"Maybe years ago, but not recently."

"Well, I do, my sweet brown eyes. You are my heart and soul, my life, my joy. I love you so much." He kissed her, and they clung together against the harshness of the world outside their love.

She walked back with him as far as her garden. "Be careful," she murmured as he paused to give her one last kiss before returning to work. "I'll worry about you now."

"Nothing's changed. Only now you know."

"Now I know." She grabbed his shirtfront. "Why didn't you tell me before? What about not having any secrets?"

He looked sheepish, his eyes flashing the reflection of the summer sky. "It was no secret." He shrugged. "But I'm glad you know. It makes me feel—I don't know—like finally someone is on my side. But I would never have told you."

"Why not?"

"I could never figure out how. And I learned to live with it long ago. I try not to think about it any more than I have to."

"I understand. And I forgive you this time. But remember—no more secrets." She shook him a little.

He straightened and looked down at her. "You too, Mrs. Brown."

She leaned away, still within the confines of his arms. "Me? I have no secrets." In his arms the fear that often haunted her as to whether he loved her above all else faded out of sight, so it didn't count.

His eyes darkened. "I think you would keep a secret from me if you thought to tell me would hurt me in some way." When she would have argued, he raised his eyebrows. "Did you not do that when you kept back the knowledge of how Lena was treating you?"

"I suppose you're right, though I hate to admit it."

He grinned. "Confession is good for the soul."

"If you say so."

He chuckled and pulled her against his chest. "Things will work out somehow. After all, don't we pray together every night for God to reveal His plan for us?"

"Umm." She doubted her faith would ever be as strong as his.

He gave her one more lingering kiss. "Now back to work I go." He tweaked her nose and strode away, stopping twice to wave at her.

She watched him disappear around the barn, a sudden lump of dread almost choking her. She strained to catch any sound of fighting but heard nothing. Still she watched, her neck growing stiff with tension. Kingston came back around the barn, looked up, saw her still there, and gave her a boisterous wave. Suddenly weak, she sank to the ground. *God, keep him safe. And please help us find a place to live.*

The prayer had been automatic. The cry of her desperate heart. Otherwise, she reasoned, she wouldn't have asked for a place to live. She'd promised Kingston she would be content to live with his family. But how she ached for a place where she and Kingston could find peace and privacy.

"Just a room alone somewhere," she whispered.

Suppertime approached. Maryelle did her best to help despite Lena's angry looks and Katherine's docile following of Lena's lead. Mother Brown kept her back turned, stirring a pan of gravy with complete indifference.

Maryelle helped Lily set the table.

"My kittens are growing up so fast," Lily announced to everyone in the room.

Katherine stopped slicing bread. "When can I see them?"

Lena lowered her gaze to Lily. For the first time, Maryelle saw a softening in Lena's expression.

"I could show you after supper." Lily sounded uncertain, and Maryelle wondered if this child had escaped Lena's harshness.

Katherine shot a look at Lena, as though wondering if her older sister would be angry. Then she turned back to Lily and said, "As soon as the dishes are done then?"

"Okay." Lily looked relieved. She turned to Lena. "You can come too."

At first Maryelle thought Lena would refuse, but then she smiled, transforming her face into soft, young lines. "Okay." She glanced at Maryelle before she turned her back.

Maryelle knew she was being snubbed. Katherine glanced from one to the other as if uncertain whether she should invite Maryelle to go with them; then, letting her shoulders sag, she returned to her task.

Maryelle turned to fill the glasses with water. Little did Lena know she'd already seen the kittens. She thought again how much younger Lena looked when she smiled. It seemed the whole family lived with unhappy secrets weighing them down. She glanced at Mother Brown's back and wondered what secrets kept her shut up inside so that she ignored the undercurrents at work around her. Was it possible she knew how her husband treated Kingston? How could she ignore it if she did?

The men thumped into the house.

Maryelle stiffened. She had not seen Father Brown since witnessing his attack on Kingston, and she wasn't sure if she could act normal.

He strode into the room followed by Angus and Kingston.

Lily bounced up to Angus's side. "You want to come with us to see the new baby kittens?"

Angus kept his head lowered, darting a glance at his father, and seeing no response in his father's face, mumbled agreement.

Lily paused before Kingston; but before she could ask him, he ruffled her hair. "I've got things to do," he said.

"Just be sure and keep them out of my way," Father Brown muttered as he pulled out his chair and sat down. "Only thing cats are good for is keeping the mice down."

Maryelle gave Lily a sympathetic glance, but the child seemed unaffected by her father's attitude.

Maryelle wished she could be as easy about the head of the house. Nothing was different in the way he spoke or acted. Still part comrade, part ruler. But every time he spoke, she twitched.

Kingston, at her side, took her hand beneath the table and squeezed it. She held on, drawing strength from his steady calmness. How he could act as if nothing had happened was beyond her ken.

❧

The crops had been planted. Kingston had put in long hours in the fields. It seemed he barely finished planting before he turned his time and attention to cutting hay.

School ended, and Jeanie was home full time, claiming much of Lily's time that Maryelle had previously enjoyed.

She was thankful the garden took more attention. The grass was determined to retain its hold and Maryelle equally determined to conquer it. The plants fought to establish themselves. Maryelle plucked every weed.

She stood back from hoeing and admired the neat rows.

Kingston, at her side, put his arm around her. "It's a fine garden, Mrs. Brown."

"Not so bad for my first attempt."

Angus edged into sight.

"Hey, Brother, isn't this a nice garden?" Kingston called.

Angus moved closer. He gave the plants a quick look before he answered. "She sure spends a lot of time out here."

Maryelle chuckled. "Because I like my garden."

Angus slipped a quick look at her. Of all Kingston's siblings, Angus remained the most distant. She had barely heard a dozen words from him.

"It looks real nice," he mumbled before he hurried away.

But the garden could not account for every hour in the day, so Maryelle went on long walks, many of which took her to the top of the hill behind the house, where she could see down the road toward town.

On several occasions she noticed Lena slip away from the house in the middle of the afternoon and hurry down the lane. Every time she turned left and walked to the place where another road branched to the south, and there she stood motionless for some time before making her way back home.

Father Brown had commented on Maryelle's wanderings. "Be careful, young lady, that you don't go roaming into trouble." Maryelle didn't know if he meant it kindly or otherwise. Since she'd seen his actions toward Kingston, she'd had a hard time thinking he could be kind.

Later, when she asked Kingston about it, he'd said, "He's just warning you to be cautious. Stay away from the cows and watch for other dangers." She pressed him further, but he couldn't be more specific.

But now she headed out behind the barn, a direction she had avoided since witnessing the scene with Father Brown brandishing the spanner at Kingston and spewing vindictive words. Not that she hadn't been drawn in that direction. There were many groves of trees, and the land rolled like a wrinkled carpet. She longed to explore. She was getting as bad as Lily at seeking out places of solitude.

For an hour or more, she wandered among the trees, going from one bunch to another. Suddenly she came upon a cluster of buildings half hidden by trees and stared at the serene setting.

"Come in for a visit." A gentle voice came from the shade beside the house.

She moved forward as a tiny woman, soft gray hair wound into a bun at the back of her head, stepped into the sunlight.

"I didn't mean to intrude," Maryelle said.

"Intrude. Pshaw. I'm glad as can be for any sort of company. Now you come on in and sit a bit."

"You're very kind." Maryelle followed her indoors, glad of some sort of diversion on this long afternoon.

The older woman waved her toward a chair and filled the kettle with water. "I'm sorry. I forgot to introduce myself. I'm Mrs. Wells."

Maryelle gave her name. "I had no idea we had such close neighbors. You're English, aren't you?"

"Oh, my, yes. Wes and I came to Canada as newlyweds. Forty years ago that was."

The house was warm and inviting, lacey antimacassars on the backs of the stuffed chairs, framed photos crowding the surfaces of the tables and sideboard.

Mrs. Wells saw her glance around the room and picked up a photo. "Here we are fresh off the boat."

The picture showed a very young couple in front of a low building that bore no resemblance to this small house.

"That's the bunkhouse out back. We lived in it for five years and then built this house. We used it as a bunkhouse for our hired men for years, but it has stood empty since the war took away all the young men."

She chose another photo and showed Maryelle. A small child stood between a slightly older Mr. and Mrs. Wells.

"This is your son?"

"That's our Harry."

"Where is he now?"

"Our Harry died." She showed Maryelle a photo of a young man probably in his early twenties. "Pneumonia took him almost fifteen years ago."

Maryelle murmured her condolences.

"There's only me and Wes now." The older woman turned toward the door as an elderly man with a firm step came into the room. "Here he is now."

"Wes, Dear, this is our new neighbor, Maryelle Brown, young Kingston's wife."

"The lad got married?"

"I told you that. Remember? She's from London."

"Have we been to London?"

The man looked from his wife to Maryelle, his expression troubled.

"Oh, my, yes, but so many years ago it's like another life."

She turned to Maryelle. "We were married in London."

Maryelle smiled. Despite the old man's fading memory, this older couple had a sweetness about them that tugged at her thoughts. "I barely remember my grandparents, but you remind me of them."

"Well, bless your heart, Child. Why don't you call us Grandma and Grandpa? We'll never have anyone of our own to call us that."

Maryelle readily agreed. It was like touching home again. She didn't realize how much she'd missed the sound of English voices, nor how lonely she'd been with no one but Kingston to show her kindness.

"You'll stay for a cup of tea, won't you?"

Maryelle laughed. "I'd love to. It's so good to hear familiar accents again."

"When I heard Kingston was bringing a British bride, I wondered how you would adjust."

"I'm adjusting."

Grandma nodded. "It's a hard time for everyone. So many of the lads died in the trenches and then that dreadful Spanish influenza." She patted Grandpa's hand. "At least we were spared that, weren't we, Dear?"

"Yes, Dear," the elderly man said. "So young Kingston's back. How is he doing?"

"Busy with farm work."

"The farm missed him."

Maryelle knew what he meant. Kingston had said much the same.

Mr. Wells finished his tea and wandered back outside, Grandma's eyes following him until he was out of sight.

"I expect you've found many things different here?"

"I couldn't believe it at first. They grow or make everything themselves."

"You learn to do what needs to be done, especially when there's no choice. You won't find a baker or butcher around here. I expect you've already learned to do many of the necessary tasks."

Maryelle ducked her head without answering.

"Tsk. Seems I've hit a troubled spot. Having difficulty learning some of the things?"

Maryelle shook her head. "No. I'm sure I could learn whatever I need to, but I'm not allowed to."

"Not allowed. What do you mean?"

"Every time I try to help, the task is snatched away. They make it clear they don't need or want my help."

"My dear."

"Oh, I help with dishes now, though it took several days before I was granted the right."

"I don't understand. Mrs. Brown has always been most efficient. I'm sure she's trained her own daughters well."

"It isn't Mother Brown." She didn't intend to say anything more; but once started, it seemed she couldn't stop. She told how Lena treated her and that everyone, except Kingston and Lily, seemed to resent and oppose her.

"I think the good Lord sent you to me so I could help you."

"You have already. I needed someone to talk to."

"I have in mind a whole lot more than that. First, we will take it to the Lord. He needs to do some healing in that family."

She took Maryelle's hands and prayed. "Lord, grant us wisdom in this situation. Strengthen Maryelle's heart. Help me find ways to ease her situation. And, dear Lord, You know the hurts in that family, especially young Lena's loss. Reach into that poor heart and flood it with Your love. Amen."

Maryelle kept her head bowed a moment longer. Grandma's prayers were like a healing balm to her soul.

Grandma pushed to her feet. "Come along now. I'll show you the place first."

They went outside. Grandma pointed out the chicken coop and the old bunkhouse and led her to the garden.

"There's Wes." Grandpa Wells bent over a piece of machinery. "Wes, what are you doing, Dear?"

"Can't get this thing to work."

They went over to see what was the problem. He had dropped some bolts on the ground. Grandma picked them up and handed them to him. "Put these in here." She pointed. "Then turn this over." She touched a handle. "See if that helps."

He nodded and did as she said, smiling when it worked.

Too soon it was time for Maryelle to go.

"I have a plan," Grandma said. "You come back early tomorrow afternoon, and I'll give you a lesson in making bread. We'll soon have you ready to run a house on your own."

Maryelle wanted to tell her that a house of her own was not in the immediate future, but she'd already said too much.

"I'll be back," she promised

Humming, she headed home. She set the table and helped serve up the food, ignoring Lena's flashing looks. She could hardly wait for supper to be over so she could tell Kingston about her afternoon.

But when the men tramped through the door, she glanced up and saw Kingston's dark expression. Her heart dropped like a rock. Father Brown glowered at Kingston's back.

Angus turned, and she noticed a smudge on one cheek.

Or was it a bruise?

But Angus ducked away before she could decide.

She silently sought Kingston's eyes, wanting to assure herself he was okay. He barely tipped his head to answer her silent inquiry.

She ached to be alone with him so they could discuss it.

Talk during the meal was left mostly to Lily and Jeanie. The others all seemed to sense things were not quite right.

Maryelle jumped up as soon as was polite, poured hot water into the basin, and began to collect and wash dishes. Kingston waited, pretending to read a paper, even though Father Brown had left again to do more work.

Angus cast a nervous look at Kingston before following his father outdoors.

Finished, Maryelle threw the dishcloth over the basin. "All done."

"Let's go for a walk." Kingston folded the paper and dropped it into the basket where the newspapers were kept.

He took her hand and strode in the direction of the garden. She practically had to trot to keep up to his long strides but said nothing, sensing he was upset.

They reached the garden without either speaking, but rather than sit on the ground as they customarily did, Kingston leaned against a tree. She stood facing him, her hand still caught in his.

"Kingston, whatever is the matter?"

His eyes shifted color as he studied her. "Ah, my sweet brown eyes, what have I brought you to?"

She had no idea what he meant but went readily into his embrace, resting her cheek against his chest, enjoying the salty smell of a hard afternoon's work.

He rubbed his hand up and down her back. She waited, knowing he would speak when he was ready. In the meantime, she leaned against him, knowing he drew comfort from her closeness even as she did from his gentle touch.

Finally his hand grew still. "I always thought it was only me."

"Only you?"

His chest rose and fell in a deep sigh. "Only me my dad treated like that."

She grew very still, her insides growing brittle as old paper. "What happened?"

"We were trying to get the rake to work. I suspect Angus caught a rock in it. Anyway, everything seemed bent and out of order. My guess is it's needed fixing since last season or longer." He let out a huge gust of air. "Dad lost his patience and cuffed Angus across the face. You saw the bruise."

She nodded, her insides screaming.

"He said we were both a pair of useless—never mind what he said."

She hugged him so hard her arms ached.

"Angus took off running as if the devil had him by the leg."

"I expect it felt like that to him."

"I grabbed Dad's arm and held it like a vise. I said, 'If you ever touch that boy again or anyone else in this family, I will personally break both your arms.' " A shudder ripped across his shoulders. "I threw his arm away and went after Angus."

"Poor Angus."

"I found him behind the pigpen. He wouldn't look at me or talk to me at first. I'm pretty sure he was crying and didn't want me to see."

"The poor boy."

"I sat down beside him and started to talk. I said I'd never have left him to go to war if I thought Dad would ever touch him."

Maryelle knew Kingston wouldn't have had a choice. If he hadn't signed up on his own, he would have been conscripted.

"I told him if Dad ever touched him again he was to come to me and I would deal with our father." For a moment he said no more, but Maryelle sensed by his tension that he wasn't through. "After awhile, I asked if Dad had done this before. At first I didn't think he was going to answer; then he mumbled, 'A time or two. Mostly he uses his boots on me.' I tell you, I saw red. To think I've put up with him all these years thinking it was only me. Letting it go because I figured as long as he had me around to turn on, he would leave the others be."

"No wonder Angus walks around as if he's afraid."

"He is afraid—of being kicked or worse."

"Kingston, what are you going to do?"

He released her and paced away. "I don't know." He ran his hand across his hair until it sprang into tails all over his head. "I'm so mad right now I feel like walking off. Let the farm fall into rack and ruin. Serve the old man right if I leave. But what will happen to Angus?"

She heard the pain and confusion in his voice and knew how difficult this was for him.

"Would he ever hit one of the girls?" She couldn't help thinking of Lily, so much like Kingston—a fact that might be enough in itself to create a problem.

"I don't think so." He spun on his heel to face her. "That's just it, don't you see? I don't know. I didn't think he'd hit Angus, but I saw it with my own eyes."

He paced back and forth, finally pausing in front of her. She almost cried at the pain in his eyes.

"What do you think I should do?" he asked. "What should we do?"

seven

Placing her palms on either side of his face, Maryelle said, "Oh, Kingston, my dear, sweet husband. I simply do not know." Part of her wanted to say, *Walk away. Let's get a home of our own.* But where would they go? How would they live? Besides, she was truly concerned about the others. "Whatever you decide is best, I will support you in it."

He reached out for her again and enclosed her in his arms. "I suppose it isn't as hard to decide as it seems." He gave a bitter laugh. "It isn't as if we have someplace else to go. I've never looked for anything else."

"The farm is your life."

"I guess you could say that."

"Then we'll find a way to sort things out." Even as she said it, her heart nosedived to her feet. She wondered if he would ever choose to leave his home and family. She wished she had the confidence to demand he do so, but she feared he would refuse. And then she'd be faced with wondering how strong his love for her was. As long as she stayed in his arms, those doubts remained bearable.

He held her close without speaking. After a long while, he whispered, "Thank you, my sweet wife. I don't know what I would do without you."

His tight hug softened, and he chuckled once. "I seem to have gotten us into a bit of a mess, wouldn't you say?"

"I would say no such thing. You've only done what was

right and honorable. How could you know how your father would act?"

He shrugged. "I wish I could see this ending well, but somehow I don't. We'll put up with him until our dying days and then wonder why we're sour inside." She knew he meant himself and his siblings. Suddenly she felt an overwhelming sadness for this family.

"How I wish you could have known my dad. He was the finest man I ever knew—except for you, of course."

He laughed. "But of course."

"I'm sure he would have been able to advise us."

"What are we thinking?" He pressed the heel of his hand to his forehead. "I thought I'd never forget."

Maryelle shook her head in wonder.

"We will pray. Somehow God will provide an answer for our situation." He knelt on the grassy spot by the garden and prayed aloud.

"God, You have been my guide these past four years. When I knew not what to do, where to turn, even what direction to turn, You showed me the way. I ask the same of You now. Amen."

She studied his bent head. "What did you mean when you prayed that He showed you the way?"

"It was a habit I learned in the trenches. So often we couldn't tell where the enemy was or where they were coming from or even how to get away from them. But I'd pray, 'God, be my guide,' and then I'd be certain what direction I should go. The guys got so they trusted me to find the way out. 'Watch the pointer,' they'd say. I told them it wasn't that I had uncanny instincts but that I had an all-knowing God and guide."

"You never told me that before. I like it. Makes God seem so real when I think of Him always showing you the way to go. Makes me very grateful He took care of you so you could come home to me."

He sat down, his back to a tree, and stretched his legs out in front of him, then pulled her close so her back pressed into his chest. He nuzzled her hair.

"I am grateful every day that I can come home to you," he whispered. "You are my heart's desire, my joy, and the love of my life."

She tipped her head back against his shoulder, sighing her contentment as she let the remnants of her worry about his love slip away. "Have I told you how much I love you?"

"Not for a long, long time. Probably years."

She giggled. "I've only been here a few months," she protested.

"Every minute apart, even if the separation is only a field or two, is like a year or more to me." He crossed her arms around her and covered them with his hands. "Now, sweet brown eyes, tell me what you did all day. Lily informs me you were gone 'all afternoon.'"

"I almost forgot. I met our neighbors, Mr. and Mrs. Wells. They seemed to know a lot about you."

"How are they? I haven't seen them since I got back."

"They're so nice."

"I used to go over often when I was a young lad. Mr. Wells taught me some carpentry."

"Mrs. Wells—she told me to call them Grandma and Grandpa, by the way, after I said they reminded me of my own grandparents. Anyway, she said if I came back tomorrow afternoon, she would teach me how to make bread. She thinks I should be learning how to become an efficient little housewife."

"Would you like that?"

"What—to become an efficient little housewife or to learn to bake bread?"

"Yes."

She giggled. "I would like it very much."

"Which one?"

"Both."

"Then you go right ahead and do it. Mrs. Wells will be a good friend for you."

"It will be fun."

"Not near as much fun as this." He kissed her.

"Umm. This is fun." She turned and wrapped her arms around his neck to pull him close. "I like this a lot," she murmured.

"Then be quiet and let me kiss—"

She didn't let him finish speaking before she caught his lips with hers. He tumbled backward on the grass, pulling her down with him, pinning her to his chest.

The problems of the day were forgotten for the time being.

&

She hurried over to the Wellses' as soon as dinner—she still couldn't get used to the noon meal being called that—was cleaned up. The sun was hot and bright. Kingston and Father Brown had said they were in need of rain soon. She'd already seen the evidence in the wilting plants of her garden.

"Welcome, Child—I hoped you'd return."

"I could hardly wait." Her insides had been tight all morning, knowing the shameful secret of the family of which she was now a member.

"Let's get right down to business." Grandma had written out a recipe and took her step-by-step through the process.

"Tell me how you met your young man."

"He walked into my shop one rainy day seeking shelter. I took one look at him and fell head over heels in love. He was so tall and handsome in his uniform—and his eyes like the Mediterranean Sea under the summer sun.

"I think he picked my shop because it was a green grocer's. It was the closest thing to a farm he could find in London.

" 'I farm back home,' he said, running his hand along the carrots in a basket.

" 'Where's back home?' I asked.

"He said, 'A little place called Flat Rock in Alberta.'"

"I asked him to tell me about this place."

Maryelle laughed. "He did. He talked nonstop for an hour, I think. Then he turned those blue-green eyes on me and said, 'So what's a girl like you doing here?'

"First thing I know, I'd told him about growing up there, how Dad had enlisted in the army days after the war started, then my utter despair when he was killed two weeks later. I told him how Mom never got over his death and slowly faded away until she died two years later. We talked long after the rain had stopped. We talked between customers. We talked until he looked at his watch and jumped to his feet. 'I'm going to miss my train,' he said and raced out."

"I'm guessing that wasn't the last you heard from him."

"I thought it would be. I went upstairs to my empty flat that night and realized how very lonely I was. A loneliness that had been emphasized by the pleasure of talking to Kingston for several hours." She smiled, a soft feeling in her chest. "You can imagine my surprise and pleasure when a letter arrived two days later. And another every day until he arrived on my step again.

"He had several more passes. We spent every waking hour together. I showed him my favorite spots in London. We made a trip out of town." That was the time they had buried Sheba. "And then he said his unit was due to be sent to France soon. He asked if I would marry him before he left. I couldn't imagine life without him, so I agreed. We were married the next weekend. We had four wonderful days together, and then he was gone. I didn't see him again until I arrived here."

"It's obvious you love him very much."

"I would do anything for him."

Grandma's face grew serious. "Let's hope you don't have to."

Her thoughts flew to Father Brown.

Grandma's eyes narrowed, and she looked intently into Maryelle's face. "Have I struck a sour note?"

"How well do you know the family?"

"We've lived side by side since before Kingston was born. At one time his mother and I were good friends."

"What happened?"

"She got busy with her babies. It was hard for her to come and visit. I went there a few times, but somehow I never felt really welcome."

"Why not?"

"I can't really say. Your father-in-law was always friendly to me—at least on the surface—but I sensed he didn't like my presence. Tsk, Child. I shouldn't be saying this to you. They're your family now, and I'm sure you find them pleasant enough except for Lena, and we have to make allowances for her grief."

Maryelle didn't answer.

"Child, what is it?"

She hadn't intended to say anything, but her troubled thoughts would not be contained. "Father Brown isn't as kind as he seems."

Grandma Wells's mouth tightened. "No doubt you have solid reasons for your opinion."

"Very solid. I've seen him hit Kingston with a spanner. And the way he talked to him—yelled. The things he said. It was awful. And last night he hit Angus. Poor Angus. No wonder he's so withdrawn. Kingston says his father's ways don't bother him. He just stands there. But Angus—I think it's destroying him." She stared down at her hands. She wanted to keep secret the things she'd discovered, but her knowledge threatened to eat her from the inside out. "I shouldn't tell you all this."

"Your secret will be safe with me. And I will pray for a miracle in that family." She paused. "I can't say I'm surprised. I've wondered for years."

"Kingston told his father if he ever touched Angus again, he would break both his arms." The thought of violence made her feel like pitching up her dinner. "I wish there were some way out."

"What do you mean?"

"I wish we could move away and live on our own."

"I expect you could."

"No, we have no place to go. And Kingston loves that farm. It would break his heart to walk away and see it go to 'rack and ruin,' as he says. Besides, what would happen to Angus?"

"So there are valid reasons for staying?"

She nodded, misery wrapping around her heart like a hangman's noose. "I wish there was some way of stopping him." She didn't have to explain to Grandma Wells that she meant Kingston's father.

"It's dangerous to interfere with a man's family. And I suspect it might only make things worse for everyone."

"Kingston said much the same. He said his mother tried to interfere on his behalf once or twice, and it only made his father angrier, more violent."

"We must take this to the Lord in prayer. He will provide an answer. And there are a couple of young men I feel we need to lift up to Him for protection."

After Grandma's heartfelt prayer, Maryelle felt a degree better.

"Let's make the bread."

Maryelle's first loaf was crude, the next one better.

"Do you have any family left in Britain?" Grandma asked as Maryelle shaped loaves.

"Not a living soul. How about you?"

"I have an older sister and a niece and nephew."

"Have you ever been back?"

"No. We planned to but never made it. There was always something else we had to spend the money on or we couldn't spare the time."

"Do you think you'll ever go back?" Maryelle asked as she shaped the rest of the dough into rolls.

"Not now. I remember a time when it was uppermost in my mind, but after Harry died and then both sets of parents passed away, there didn't seem to be any reason. And now we're too old, and I don't think Wes could take the trip.

"There—you're done. There won't be time for you to bake them today so I'll just tell you." She explained how to test the temperature of the oven, where to place the loaves, how to tell if they were done.

Grandpa Wells wandered in then and began poking through the cupboards in the back room.

"What are you looking for, Wes?"

He came out and stared at his wife. "You know—I can't remember." He laughed. "I guess I thought I'd know when I saw it. How long 'til supper?"

"About an hour."

"Is it that time already?" Maryelle said. "I'd better get home. Thank you so much. It's been wonderful."

"Come again any time. I'd be glad to teach you whatever you like."

Maryelle paused. "Biscuits. Canadian biscuits, not our English ones. I want to know how to make those."

"Child, they're as easy as rolling off a log. Come tomorrow, and by the time you go home, you'll know how to make a light biscuit that will make your Kingston's mouth water. Why, I've won awards at the fair for years with my biscuits."

"I'll be back if it's at all possible."

"I will be praying for you."

Back home, tension returned to her muscles the minute Father Brown entered the room, Angus and Kingston at his heels.

She was certain she wasn't the only one feeling the tension. Mother Brown spent long hours at her garden. Jeanie and Lily spent most of their time at the playhouse in the trees.

Lena no longer went for walks, choosing instead to inflict her misery on the inhabitants of the house. Poor Katherine received most of it and grew more and more dependent on Lena for direction for every move.

Maryelle found solace in her solitary walks and in afternoons spent at the Wellses'.

"I've been thinking," she said one afternoon as she fried chicken for Grandma. "I think I've found a way to gain some ground at home."

"What's that, my dear?"

"Well, I think I could make bread on my own now."

"You're a quick learner."

"Thanks. I keep trying to tell Lena that."

"Sooner or later she'll realize it."

"I've decided to make it sooner. I'm going to get up early tomorrow morning and start the bread before anyone else gets up. I'll show them I can do it."

"I don't see any harm in that."

"I've thought about it, and I can't see any reason for anyone to object."

"Does there have to be a reason?"

"No." She let her shoulders slump. "But I've got to be allowed to do something."

"Then go ahead. Make a batch of nice bread. And let the bricks fall where they may."

"Ouch. That doesn't sound too good."

"My dear, don't expect instant reversal in everyone's attitudes. It will take time for the family to learn to accept you."

"I think they've had plenty of time. I've been here over three months."

"I know it must be frustrating. I've been praying for things to change. Maybe this is the way. You go ahead, Dear. No one can fault you for doing a good deed."

"I hope not." She said it with far more conviction than she felt.

She shared her plans with Kingston. "I'm going to get up early tomorrow morning," she told him as they prepared for bed. "I'm going to prove I'm capable of making bread, and it seems the only way I'll be allowed to do so is to get up before everyone else and just do it."

"You know what I like about you?"

"Everything, I would hope."

"Well, yes, but I was thinking of one thing in particular."

"And are you going to tell me what it is, Mr. Canada?"

He ran his finger down her nose. "Maybe it wouldn't be good for me to say anymore. Wouldn't want you to get a swelled head or anything."

She pounced on him, tickling him until he yelled.

"Shh. You want the whole family to come pounding on the door to see what's the matter?"

He choked back his laughter and caught her hands to stop her onslaught.

"No fair, brown eyes. Tickle me to death then tell me not to laugh."

He pulled her down on his chest and kissed her nose.

"So what was it you like about me?"

"Back then I was thinking of your fighting spirit—a real British bulldog." He cupped her face in his hands. "But right now"—his voice was low—"I'm thinking how much I like your eyes, your upturned little nose, your rosebud mouth." He proceeded to kiss her.

She waited until he broke away before she asked, "Have I told you how much I like everything about you?"

"I don't believe you have. But you could show me now and make up for neglecting to tell me."

With a happy laugh, she leaned toward him. Her heart was so full, she thought she wouldn't be able to contain the shout of joy begging to escape.

His eyes darkened to the color of old pines as she kissed him.

❧

She woke as the sun filled the sky with a pink blush. Kingston stared bleary-eyed at her as she pulled on her clothes.

"I'm going to start the bread," she whispered. "Go back to sleep."

"And miss the chance of seeing my wife being domestic? I wouldn't think of it." He stood, stretched his arms above his head, bent from side to side, and yawned loudly, then sank back to the edge of the bed.

She leaned over and kissed him. "You're bright-eyed this morning."

He groaned. "Beats me how you can spring from the bed with such clear eyes."

"I have a mission."

"Yeah, right. Make bread." He yawned again. "Don't suppose you'd consider doing it another day?"

"Hurry up, or I'll go without you."

He groped for his pants, struggled into them, and staggered after her.

Downstairs she quietly gathered up the things she needed and measured everything out as Grandma Wells had taught her. She knew she would have to wait while the dough rose, but if her calculations proved correct, she could manage to get the bread into pans before anyone else got up. To be on the safe side, she covered the bread pan and hid it in the little room that housed the cream separator.

"I'm done for now. Come on—let's go for a walk or something."

Kingston set aside the paper he'd been reading and tiptoed after her. "Why do I feel like I'm a thief in my own house?"

"Think of it as Christmas or something."

"How are you going to bake the loaves without being discovered?"

"I'm hoping I can put the dough into pans before anyone gets up." She checked the position of the sun. "I'll try to hide the loaves until they're ready to bake. Once they're in the oven, I'm home free." She giggled. "Have you thought how silly it is to be sneaking around to work?"

He took her hand and swung it as they walked. "Never thought I'd see the day."

They walked in happy silence toward the garden. "This morning was nice." He squeezed her hand. "Just the two of us together in the kitchen—you busy working, me pretending to read the paper but really watching you."

She stopped, jerking him to a halt. "You were looking at me? Whatever for?"

He tugged her arm, marching forward, not bothering to look at her as he answered. "I was enjoying the scenery."

"What scenery?" she asked.

He paused then and grinned down at her. "You, sweet Maryelle. You're the best-looking thing around here."

"Kingston, you are so sweet." She remained sober in spite of his wide grin. "I don't know how I survived without you."

"Why is that?" He waggled his eyebrows.

"Are you fishing for a compliment?"

"Shamelessly," he admitted, grinning like a satisfied cat.

"You certainly deserve it." She tipped her head. "Let me think. What is it that makes you so special?"

His expression sagged. "Is it that hard to think of something?"

"I'm only teasing. It's not hard at all. I could start with your eyes that are so beautiful and expressive. I love it when you look at me and they go all dark. I know what you're thinking without even asking."

"Is that a fact? So what am I thinking now?"

She grinned. "That you'd like to kiss me."

He turned away. "You're crazy."

"Now quit trying to distract me unless you don't want to hear any more of your praises sung."

"Sing on, dear wife; sing on."

"You are as tall and straight as a ship's mast. You are strong. You have a wonderful sense of humor. You. . ."—her voice grew husky—"you have the most wonderfully free way of saying sweet things to me. I love that about you."

"A ship's mast?"

She shrugged. "It was the first thing that came to mind."

"Tall and skinny."

"Straight, with an upright bearing."

He sighed. "Beanpole."

She groaned. "Did I mention argumentative and stubborn?"

"How did we get from I'm so special to I'm stubborn and argumentative?"

"Better ask yourself that."

"Right. Kingston, how—?"

"You are truly impossible at times."

"Yes, but you like it. You know you do."

"I give up."

"About time."

They had reached the garden. He pulled her into the crook of his arm. "Now stop being argumentative, and let us enjoy the beautiful morning."

"Umm." She nestled into his embrace. "It's nice to be the only ones up."

"We should do this more often."

She sighed. "I wish we could be alone more often."

"Me too, but I don't see how it's possible."

"Unless we have our own place." Would he listen to her request?

His arm tightened around her. "Are you regretting things?"

"Only that I can't have you to myself."

"It will come, dear sweet Maryelle. It will come."

She nodded. The promise of things to come did little to satisfy the needs and wants of the present. Yet she knew their choices were very narrow. They basically had no place else to go, and, besides, what about Angus?

"Your garden is looking fine."

"It needs rain."

"The whole country needs rain. Pray to God it comes soon. The hay crops are burning; the wheat and oats are in the boot stage and about half as high as they should be."

She knelt to examine some of her plants. "The carrots need thinning. I guess I'll do that today. But the bean plants have stopped growing altogether." She moved on to her row of vines—squash, pumpkin, and cucumbers. "If I could water these, I could salvage them."

"You could use the wash water and slop water from the house."

She stood and stared at him. "That's a good idea. I'll tell them at breakfast I want it to carry to my garden. They won't mind, will they?"

"Why should they? It's only going to be thrown out."

She knew that what he said made sense, but nothing around here ever seemed to be as simple as it should be. "I suppose we should go back. I'll put the dough in pans now and hide it before everyone gets up." She had discussed it with Grandma, who agreed that this time, in order to gain the ground she wished, she could skip a second rising.

If Kingston's parents were surprised to discover she and Kingston were up when they came from their room, they gave no indication. Then Mother Brown checked the coffeepot, and finding it full of fresh hot coffee, she looked startled. As she poured herself and her husband each a cup, she glanced around the kitchen, checking, Maryelle supposed, to see if anything else was out of the ordinary; but she had managed to hide the bread pans on the top shelf in the pantry, covered with a tea towel. Everything else was washed and returned to its rightful spot. There was nothing to indicate she'd done anything but make the coffee.

Over breakfast Maryelle announced she would like the washing-up water for her garden. No one protested. After breakfast dishes were done, she poured the water into a bucket and carried it to the garden to pour it carefully on four cucumber plants.

Later, when she was sure the loaves were rounded and ready to bake, she went to the little pantry and carried two pans out. She'd kept an eye on the stove all morning and knew the oven was hot enough. Without saying anything, she slipped two loaves into the oven and was returning for the other two. As she straightened, she came face to face with Lena.

"What are you trying to prove?" the girl demanded.

eight

"I should think that's obvious." Maryelle set aside the potholders. "I'm proving I can make bread."

"What makes you think you can make bread?"

"Why don't you wait a bit until it's done and you tell me?" Maryelle smiled at Lena, determined not to be drawn into an argument. "It will be ready for dinner."

"Humph." Lena jerked away, practically slamming her empty cup on the table. "Who says we need bread for dinner?"

"I've yet to sit down to a meal in this house where there isn't bread or biscuits on the table." She refrained from mentioning she would soon be preparing biscuits. One victory at a time.

She breathed a sigh when all four loaves came from the oven golden and well risen. They sat on the cupboard cooling when Mother Brown came in from the garden. She nodded at the freshly baked loaves, then turned to Lena. "Good. Forgot to tell you we needed bread. Glad you remembered." She drew her brows together. "You must have started early."

Lena didn't bother to correct her mother and gave Maryelle a dark look, daring her to do so. Maryelle shrugged. It didn't matter what Mother Brown thought as much as it did that she prove to Lena she could not only learn to do something, but she had every intention of doing so and pulling her share around the house.

It was Kingston who revealed the truth. He bit into a thick slice slathered with homemade butter. Maryelle eyed the butter. Another task she was determined to learn in spite of opposition.

"This is great bread, Maryelle. Don't you think so?" His question included the rest of those around the table.

"You made this?" It was Katherine who dared admit the accomplishment. "When?"

"I guess that explains what you two were doing up so early," Father Brown said. "I wondered what you were up to."

"It's good," Lily said.

Jeanie watched Lena, waiting to see her response.

Lena reached across the table for the salt, passing the bread without taking a slice. "About time she learned to do something useful."

Maryelle stared at her. "You seem to be enjoying the baby carrots I brought in from the garden. I'd say that was useful."

Lena pushed the rest of her carrots to the side of her plate. Maryelle knew they'd be going to the pigs. She bit her tongue to keep from retorting. Mother Brown said nothing, keeping her attention on her plate.

Maryelle waited, knowing the older woman would have to look up sooner or later. She finally did, a darting glance that slid away as quickly as it came but not before Maryelle caught a glimpse of—dare she believe it—understanding.

Father Brown took a slice of bread. "Food is food. Now let's eat up and get back to work. We've wasted enough time already this morning with having to fix that axle."

Maryelle's neck muscles tingled at the look he fired at Angus. She knew she didn't imagine the way the boy drew his shoulder forward. She slanted a look at Kingston. His eyes were on his brother. His jaw clenched until she knew his teeth would be ready to crack. Her appetite fled. What had happened this morning to make the brothers so uneasy?

Kingston turned toward her for a moment. His eyes were so full of pain and despair that she wanted to jump to her feet and demand answers from this family seated so quietly around the table. *What's the matter with you? Why do you have to be so cruel to each other?* But Kingston held her gaze until she calmed down. She knew without any words being exchanged that some things were best left unspoken. To voice her feelings would fuel the emotions causing the problem.

She gave an almost imperceptible shrug, and Kingston relaxed. She tried to smile at him, but all she managed was a little grimace. He seemed to understand for he tipped his head a fraction of an inch in silent acknowledgment.

"Pass me some more bread, Maryelle," Lily said.

"Please?" Mother Brown corrected.

Lily sighed. "Sorry. Forgot. Please pass the bread."

Maryelle handed her the plate, smiling at the innocent child. How long before her world was tainted with the stain of this family? She wanted more than anything in the world a place where she and Kingston could be alone, but how could she even consider leaving this child to the mercy of her cruel sisters, her angry father, and her indifferent mother? Her gaze returned to Angus, his head still bent over his plate even though his fork had not moved in several minutes. What about this poor lad? Would anyone but Kingston defend him? She doubted it. She ducked her head and shuffled two carrots around on her plate. How had she ended in such a mix-up?

"Let's get back to work." Father Brown pushed his chair away from the table, the legs scraping on the floor with a sound that sent shivers up Maryelle's spine.

Kingston paused to kiss her on the forehead and murmur for her ears only, "We'll talk later," before he tramped after his father.

Angus sighed, his shoulders lifting and falling, and pushed away from the table, his meal only partly eaten. As he passed his mother, she squeezed his hand.

It was a gesture so unexpected and quick that Maryelle wondered if she'd really seen it. But Angus carried his head a little higher as he followed the men out the door.

Maryelle listened to the conversation around her as she washed dishes, and Jeanie and Lily dried and put them away.

"It is getting awfully dry," Mother Brown said. "We need rain soon."

"I hate rain," Lena muttered.

"You do?" Katherine sounded surprised.

Maryelle watched the girls out of the corner of her eyes.

Lily leaned toward Jeanie. "I got an idea for this afternoon."

"You girls play close to the house," their mother said.

"I remember when you wished it would rain so"—Katherine swallowed hard as Lena glared at her with eyes like a small animal's—"so Eddie. . ." Her voice trailed off, and she scrubbed the table with unnecessary vigor.

"I hate rain," Lena muttered, turning to the stairs now that she was certain her sister had been quelled. Her feet thudded up the steps and across the floor overhead.

"I love dancing in the rain," Lily said to no one in particular.

Maryelle hid a smile. The child was so unspoiled. She handed the last saucepan to Jeanie and rinsed the washrag with water from the kettle as Grandma Wells had taught her. She took the tea towels from the little girls and took them outside to hang on the line. Grandma had said, "A few hours in the sunshine does wonders."

She got back to the step in time to catch Lena tossing the washing-up water out the door.

"I told you I wanted the water for my garden."

Lena shrugged. "I forgot."

"I rather doubt you forgot. Why don't you spare me your vindictiveness?"

Lena fixed her with her dark eyes. "Why don't you go back where you belong?"

Maryelle took a deep breath and tried to contain her anger. "And where would that be?"

"London. Go home, English prissy. Go home."

Maryelle held her stance. "I have no home in London as you very well know. Besides, what would you suggest I do about my marriage to Kingston?"

"Take him with you."

Tears stung her eyes, but Maryelle was too angry to cry. She wanted to shake this girl until her beady little eyes rolled to the ground. "I hate to break this to you, Lena Brown, but you aren't the only one who lost loved ones in the war. Only not everyone let it turn them into a sour, bitter shrew."

"And what gives you the right to be my judge and jury?"

"You do, every time you turn your bitter tongue on me or on someone else in this family who is less capable of withstanding your vitriolic behavior."

"What happens in this family has nothing to do with you."

"That's where you're wrong. I *am* a part of this family. You might as well learn to live with it."

"Never." She fairly spat the word out. "And if you think you can worm your way in by baking a few loaves of bread, forget it." She breathed hard. "As to your garden, well, this is what I think of you and your precious garden." She shook the last drops of water from the dishpan, tucked it under her arm, and stormed into the house.

Maryelle looked after her, her insides shaking. How could she live here with Lena's hatred and the overshadowing fear of Father Brown's anger?

Spinning away, she ran toward the only place she could find comfort—Grandma Wells's.

By the time she reached the boundary between the two farms, she had such a stitch in her side, she ran bent to one side, her hand pressed into her gut, trying to ease the pain. Her steps slowed to a ragged trot.

She didn't bother to knock but pushed the door open and stood before Grandma, her hands on her knees, panting like a dog.

"Child, did you run all the way over?"

Maryelle nodded her head, too winded to speak.

"I expect you had some reason?"

Maryelle gave a crooked smile. Grandma's voice said she doubted there was reason enough to act as Maryelle had.

Finally she was able to suck in enough oxygen to stop the pounding in her head and collapsed on one of Grandma's wooden chairs with its braided round seat cover.

"I had to get away."

Grandma clucked sympathetically. "What's happened?"

Too miserable to sort out her words, Maryelle let them pour out. "It's nothing new. Lena spared no words in telling me she thought I should get out and take Kingston with me. And dinner was strained. It was obvious Father Brown had one of his moods this morning. Both Angus and Kingston were subdued." She stopped to catch her breath. "How could she say that about Kingston? That hurts more than anything."

"My dear. It seems things are going from bad to worse."

"I wonder how much more I can take."

"What are your options?"

Maryelle slumped over the table. "I don't see what options we have, but I don't see how Kingston can stand it."

Grandma took her hands. "Perhaps it seems normal to him."

She jerked her head up. "How can it seem normal to anyone?"

"It's always been his family, remember. And didn't you say his father has always treated him harshly?"

Her face went cold. "I can't imagine putting up with this all your life."

"It's not what God intended." Grandma looked thoughtful. "I've been praying about this a lot and asking God what His solution is for this situation. I can't help wondering if He's set you in this place so you could help."

"Help," Maryelle whispered. "How could I possibly help? Whatever I try to do is thrown back in my face." Baking bread had been an unsatisfying victory.

"I know that. That isn't the sort of help I was thinking of."

Maryelle waited, wondering what she meant.

"I know you're especially concerned about the younger children. Maybe you're there for their sake."

"But what can we possibly do? Both Father Brown and Lena would most certainly react badly if they thought I was interfering in some way."

Grandma lifted her hands in defeat. "I don't have the answers. Only God does. I firmly believe He will reveal them in His time."

Maryelle sighed. "I certainly hope so. There are days when

I am actually afraid. I think I'm more nervous here than I was in London during the war."

Grandma took her hand between her soft palms. "If you ever need a place of safety, Child, you are welcome here. Both you and Kingston. In fact, that's part of what God has been bringing to mind." She pushed to her feet. "Come. I have something to show you."

Maryelle followed her out the door, past the garden where Grandpa Wells stood leaning on his hoe staring off across the field, past the rows of cherry trees, past the gnarled apple tree, until they reached a low narrow building Grandma had called the bunkhouse. Grandma opened the door and stepped inside.

It was a long one-roomed house. Dappled light came through the wide windows along the south wall. A bed stood at one end. In the middle of the room, across from where Maryelle stood next to Grandma, a table and two wooden rockers stood before a fieldstone fireplace. The far end held a stove and a row of shelves.

"This is where Wes and I lived for five years. Harry was born here." She ran a white hand along the tabletop. "For years our various hired men lived here." She faced Maryelle. "I haven't said anything. I haven't wanted to interfere. But if you and Kingston ever need it, this place is available."

A sob shuddered over Maryelle's lips, and then she swallowed hard. "I'd move in here today if Kingston would agree," she mumbled.

"You must follow his lead," Grandma warned. "I'm sure he knows what's best for everyone."

Maryelle nodded. "He's concerned about Angus. He feels he has to protect him."

"That makes sense, doesn't it?"

Maryelle wished she could argue, but Grandma was right. "I will do my best to be satisfied with living under the same roof as the rest of the family." It would be extremely hard now that she'd seen a means of escape. "But I'm going to mention this place to Kingston, if you don't mind. Perhaps he'd be willing to move out if he could still be close enough to help his father."

"You go right ahead, my dear. And we will pray for God's guidance." She pulled out one chair for herself and indicated Maryelle should take the other; and in that little one-roomed house with dust motes floating in the patches of light, Grandma prayed for wisdom and courage for Maryelle and Kingston.

Maryelle stayed for tea, but she could hardly wait to return home. At her first opportunity, she was going to tell Kingston about the offer of a house at the Wellses'. Perhaps he would agree it was best to move out.

She hummed and skipped her way home.

She passed the last bunch of trees and saw Kingston carrying something toward the barn. There was no sign of Angus or his father.

"Kingston, wait up."

He turned at her call. Even across the distance, she could see his eyes flash green. He smiled as she ran toward him. Simply the sight of him was enough to fill her with gladness and excitement. The possibility of a home of their own sent her pulse into a full-blown gallop.

"You look happy today," he said as she drew closer.

She pretended to pout. "Are you inferring that I'm usually down in the mouth?"

"Course not." He planted a kiss on her nose. "Have you been to see Grandma Wells?"

"Yes, and I have wonderful news." She glanced around to make sure they were alone. "What are you doing?"

"Putting this stuff away." He lifted the bundle of tools.

"I have the best news." She pranced on her tiptoes before him. "I've found us a place to live."

His arms fell to his side. "I don't understand."

"Grandma Wells has a little house she will let us live in. It's perfect. It's close enough for you to come over to work. But, think of it, we can be on our own. It's perfect."

A thud sounded from the barn. Maryelle gulped. "What was that?"

"Dad is in there." Kingston's jaw muscles corded.

"I thought you were alone," she whispered.

"Run along to the house. We'll discuss this later."

She ran as if a hundred vicious dogs were at her heel. She didn't know why she should be so stirred up inside. What did it matter if Father Brown overheard her? Yet she was worried and so scared, her mouth tasted like sawdust.

Her worries were for nothing, she decided, as supper progressed with no more and no less than its usual tension and undercurrents.

Angus ate more supper than he had dinner. Maryelle took it as a sign things had gone better in the afternoon. When Father Brown seemed more jovial than usual, she pushed aside the cable of tension that had gripped her since she'd spilled her message to Kingston an hour ago.

"I'm taking this water to my garden," she said to Kingston. She knew enough now to keep her hands on the basin until the water was safely rationed out to her plants.

"I'll take it for you." He carefully measured the water out on her squash plants under her watchful eye.

"If only it would rain," she muttered. "Is it always like this?"

"Usually we complain it rains so much we can't get the hay up. This spell will likely end soon. I hope before the crops suffer too much." He turned the basin upside down in the grass and pulled her into his arms. "I don't know what I'd do without you," he whispered against her hair.

"You'd do." She clung to him, letting the aches and troubles of the day slip away in the consolation of his embrace. "Besides, are you planning to do away with me?"

His arms tightened around her until she moaned.

"Sorry. Didn't mean to hurt you. But even the thought of something happening to you is more than I can stand."

"Then don't think it. I plan to be right here for a long time." She tapped his chest to indicate she meant here, in his arms. "Tell me what happened earlier today."

He sighed and lifted his head. "Nothing new. Dad lost his patience and tried to boot Angus. I stepped in and stared him down. I didn't say anything. Didn't need to. But it put him in a foul mood the rest of the day. He doesn't like to be interfered with."

She shook her head. "Poor Angus."

"I worry about Angus. I learned never to show fear. I discovered it fueled his anger. But every time Dad starts to roar, Angus looks like he's going to cry."

A heavy weight seemed to drop to Maryelle's feet. "You would never feel right about leaving Angus to face your father alone, would you?"

"Someone needs to protect him."

"There's no point in mentioning Grandma Wells's offer, is there?" Mentally she bid a painful farewell to the little house Grandma Wells had offered.

"I'm sorry." She felt his pain. "I'm sure it won't be forever."

"It will be over by Christmas?" She echoed a phrase every-one had said at the beginning of the war.

He stiffened, understanding her meaning.

"It went on for four long, bloodstained years." What she didn't say, but what they both understood, was the unspoken question: Would this be long, pain-filled years? "I didn't think I would survive it." *I'm not sure I can survive a long siege of this.*

"What would you have me do?" It was a cry for help.

"I don't know. I simply don't know," she whispered against his chest, clinging to his shirtfront with both fists.

He sat on the ground, pulling her into the shelter of his body so he almost engulfed her. His bent legs formed two walls of shelter; his arms wrapped around the front until she was lost in his warmth; his breath the very air she inhaled; the rise and fall of his chest, the impetus for her own breathing.

"Maryelle," he groaned. "I feel as if I'm trapped. If I stay, you pay the price; if I leave, I suspect Angus will pay a hefty price."

"I think I can better withstand the storms than he can." Angus looked and acted as if he was already close to defeat. She sighed her acceptance. "I can put up with it if you can."

He buried his face in her neck. "I don't know how I'd sur-vive without you."

"You'd survive," she muttered. Suddenly a black specter flit-ted through her mind. "I'd not make it without you though."

"You'd make it."

She shook her head. "Don't say that. I wouldn't." She knelt before him and grabbed his shoulders. "You are all I have." Whatever they had to endure was nothing compared to the thought of somehow losing him. She promised herself she would ignore Lena, or anything else that might rear its ugly head, in order to be at Kingston's side. Closing her eyes, she lowered her head and unerringly found his lips.

He tumbled backward, laughing. She lay sprawled across his chest. She could no longer reach his lips, and he grinned down at her. "Have I told you how much I love you, Mrs. Brown?"

They slipped into the house much later and, avoiding the others, hurried up the stairs to the privacy of their room.

Maryelle watched her husband unbutton his shirt and pull it over his head, then reached out and tickled his sides. With his arms trapped in the shirt and his head hidden inside it, he had little chance to defend himself.

"Maryelle," he grunted, jerking back, almost losing his balance. "Stop that."

He wriggled madly, freeing himself from the restricting garment. He stepped back and scowled at her. "Get ready for bed."

Laughing, she turned to lift her nightgown from the peg next to the stacked trunks, her glance sliding over the pictures displayed there. She gasped and leaned closer, the nightgown forgotten.

Frantically she searched the top of the trunk, lifting each framed picture and finally the runner. "It's gone." She spun around to face Kingston. "It's gone."

"What's gone?"

"My picture of Sheba."

"You're quite sure?"

"Of course. It's always right here." She patted the empty spot. "I look at it every morning and night to give myself a friendly little boost. It was here this morning."

He turned her away from her endless searching and pulled

her into his arms. "It will show up."

Her mouth against his chest, she mumbled, "Why would anyone take it? It doesn't make sense."

He shrugged. "I'm beginning to think nothing around here makes sense anymore." He gently led her to the bed, easing her out of her shift and into her nightgown. "It's been a long day. Let's go to bed and forget about it." He lay down beside her and pulled her against him. "Things will look better in the morning."

"I hope so." There was a dreadful ache behind her eyes. For a day that had begun so full of promise, it certainly had ended on a sour note. She clung to the comfort of Kingston's solidness. Long after his breathing deepened, she lay staring into the darkness, wondering how a man as gentle and fine as Kingston could have sprung from such a family.

⋈

She woke the next morning with eyes that felt as if she'd stood out in a sandstorm. She moaned as she hung her nightgown on the hook and again saw the empty spot where Sheba's picture belonged.

"Maryelle, my sweet," Kingston said, "try not to think about it. Do you have other pictures of her?"

"It was my favorite."

"I'll ask if anyone knows what happened to it."

Lena was the only person who would be so vindictive. She made no secret of how she felt. "Don't bother. Do you really expect someone to pop up and say, 'Oh, I borrowed it. Sorry. Here you are'?" If her suspicions were correct, the best thing she could do was ignore it.

She sat through breakfast without once looking at Lena, grateful for the frequent touch of Kingston's hand on her neck. As soon as the dishes were done, she grabbed the water and headed for the garden, walking slowly and carefully to avoid spilling it. She reached the edge of the garden and lifted her eyes.

"No!" She dropped the basin, not caring about the water sloshing over her shoes and soaking her skirt. Her garden was churned up as if someone had taken a plow to it; deep hoof tracks trailed back and forth. One moist, smelly cow pie covered one of her precious squash plants.

nine

She fell to her knees and plucked from the quagmire a trampled pea vine, chewed up like an old toothpick. She edged along the row. What wasn't ground into the soil was torn up, roots exposed to the air. She leaned back and moaned, then scrambled to her feet and raced the length of the garden, looking for some reason to hope. At the end she collapsed in the rough soil. Not one live plant. All her hard work for nothing.

She lifted her face to the heavens and let out an agonized wail. Was there nothing in this place that she could hold on to and call her own? Her efforts to belong were thrown back in her face; her picture of Sheba was missing; and now her garden was totally destroyed. She bowed her forehead to the ground. All she had left was her love for Kingston, and sometimes she wondered if she was losing him to his family.

It was too much. She couldn't take anymore. She fell face down and sobbed for all the things she'd lost—her father and mother, her dreams, a home where she belonged. She had nothing left to hope in. She was defeated. No more fight left. She sobbed until she was empty inside; then she lay there, face down in her misery, too broken to get up.

She heard the grass rustle nearby, but she didn't bother to look up. They had broken her. It mattered not if they saw her in utter ruin and defeat.

A pair of warm, familiar hands touched her shoulders. She didn't move. She wanted nothing but to lie where she was until all feeling ceased.

"Come on, Maryelle." Kingston pulled her to her feet, turning her into his embrace. "How long have you been lying here?"

She couldn't answer but lay limp against him.

"Good thing Lily saw you and came and got me."

She heard the tightness in his voice but didn't know or care what it meant.

"I've had enough," he said as he lifted her into his arms and strode to the house. He crashed through the door and with his boot snagged a chair toward him, lowering her carefully to it.

"Get me some warm water," he bellowed at someone.

Maryelle caught a fleeting glimpse of Lena's startled face and then a basin of water was placed close by.

He lifted her chin and gently touched her cheek with the cloth. His gaze found hers, and he paused, deep troubled thoughts turning his eyes a hard green. Then he smiled slowly. "No more of this, I promise."

The door banged. Maryelle recognized Father Brown's footsteps and shrank back. Kingston put his arm around her shoulders, pressing her to his side.

She leaned against him, refusing to look into the unkind faces of his family.

"Dad." Kingston's voice was hard. "The cows have been deliberately chased across Maryelle's garden. It's destroyed."

She heard the silent accusation of his words and knew he thought his father had done it even as she thought it.

She'd feared something would happen ever since she knew he'd overheard her suggestion to Kingston that they leave.

She held her breath and waited for him to admit or deny it, but he didn't say a word.

She felt Kingston shift as he looked around the room. "You have all gone out of your way to make Maryelle unwelcome. But you forget one thing. I love her, and when you hurt her, you hurt me." His hands tightened around her shoulders. "I will not allow her to be treated like this any longer." He faced his father boldly. She felt him pull himself up tall. "We'll be moving on."

She jerked her head up so she could see her husband. His jaw was rigid, the skin around his eyes taut. She had never seen him look so stern.

"Boy, you walked away from this place once before. Don't figure you can do it again and come back."

Maryelle shuddered before the vile tone of Father Brown's voice.

"Whatever you want," Kingston said.

Mother Brown was just behind her husband, and she glowered at his back. "He's my son too. He'll always find a welcome in my home."

The older man swung around, his fist raised to his side. For a moment Maryelle thought he would strike his wife.

Kingston dropped his arm from around her shoulders, leaving a sudden chill. She felt him surge forward, then ease back as his father dropped his fist, growling low in his throat.

Maryelle caught a movement out of the corner of her eye, turned, and saw Lena step protectively toward her mother. Maryelle blinked. She hadn't expected Lena to care about anyone else.

As she dragged her gaze back toward the older man, she saw Angus drawn back into the corner, his eyes big as plates. His gaze caught and held hers. She ached at the fear and despair she saw. How would he manage without Kingston to defend him? A shudder started in the soles of her feet and raced upward, shaking her entire frame.

Kingston leaned toward her, pulling her close, his touch lending her strength.

"Maryelle, run up and pack your things."

Her legs felt as foreign as the new country to which she'd been transplanted as she stumbled up the stairs. In a few minutes she had thrown everything back into the trunk. What didn't fit and the bulk of Kingston's belongings she tossed into the middle of the quilt and tied the corners together.

Weakness swept through her, and she sank to the floor, pressing her hand to her mouth to hold back the nausea.

Kingston found her there and sank down to her side, cradling her in his arms. "My sweet Maryelle, what have I brought you to?"

She shook her head. "It's not your fault."

He lifted his shoulders. "I thought things would get better, not worse."

"Me too." She clung to him, pressing her face into his warm neck.

"I hope Grandma Wells meant it when she offered the bunkhouse."

She nodded. "She meant it."

"Then that's where we'll go." Although she clung to him, he pushed her back to look into her face.

"I have never been so angry in my whole life as I was when I saw you weeping on the ground." A shudder raced across his shoulders.

"I wasn't hurt, not physically. Only shocked at the vindictiveness of it." She pushed back the hurt and pain. There was nothing to be gained by reliving those awful moments.

"Is everything ready to go?"

She nodded toward the bed.

"We'll take the bundle with us. I'll come and get the rest later."

She grabbed his shirtfront. "I can't bear to think of you coming back here. What if your father—?"

He drew himself up tall. "I have never been afraid of him. I'm not going to start now."

She sagged against him. "I'm afraid of him."

"Never let it show."

He scooped the bundle off the bed and, taking her hand, headed for the stairs.

His father was gone when they stepped into the kitchen. Lena sat at the table, her face turned away. She resolutely refused to look at them.

Katherine stood at the cupboard, misery written all over her features.

Mother Brown stirred a pot on the stove, turning as they entered the room. For a moment Maryelle thought she was going to ignore them and let them leave without saying a word. But suddenly, strength that seemed unfamiliar found its way into her. "I would change things if I could, but he's not getting any easier to live with." Her shoulders slumped in defeat as she let her gaze rest on Maryelle briefly. "I regret how we've treated you." She turned back to the stove.

Maryelle looked around for Angus. He still leaned in the dark corner against the pantry. She was certain he hadn't moved since they'd left the room.

Kingston strode to his side, squeezing his shoulder.

Angus shuddered like a building hit by a bomb.

"Angus, if he ever touches you, come and get me. I'll not allow it."

The boy lifted his head, clinging to Kingston's gaze like a man offered a reprieve from the gallows.

"I mean it, Angus. Don't be afraid anymore."

The door flew open, crashing into the wall, and two small bodies burst through. Lily was first. She skidded to a stop.

"Where you going?" Her gaze darted to Maryelle. "I thought you was staying forever."

Maryelle blinked back tears. How she hated to leave this little girl, so much like Kingston in looks and spirit, but she had no choice.

Maryelle squatted so she was level with the child's eyes. "We aren't going far. There's a little house at Mr. and Mrs. Wells's that we're going to live in for now. It's close enough so you can come and visit"—she sought Mother Brown's eyes—"as long as you have permission from your mother first." She turned to Jeanie, who stood uncertainly inside the door. "You too, Jeanie."

Maryelle stood. "All of you." But her voice faltered. Jeanie looked around the room, trying to gauge the feeling by the adults' expressions. Maryelle knew she wasn't sure how she should react.

Kingston stepped toward the door, holding his hand out to Maryelle. "I wish things could be different." He took Maryelle's hand and paused as if waiting for some sort of reply from his family. But no one spoke.

Maryelle followed him out the door. Perhaps everything that could be said had been said.

Lily burst out the door. "Don't go!" she cried.

Kingston stopped, filling his lungs slowly. He glanced at Maryelle, his eyes shifting to blue, revealing his pain; and lowering the bundle, he turned toward his littlest sister.

"Come here, Sweetie."

Lily flew into his arms. She was crying, her tears dripping off her chin.

"Don't cry, Lily."

Maryelle swallowed back her own tears.

"I don't want you to go," she sobbed.

"I know," he crooned, cradling the child's head close. "But we have to." He set her down. "You be a good girl."

He grabbed Maryelle's hand, squeezing tight. "Let's go," he muttered, striding from the yard so fast she was forced to trot to keep up.

They went several hundred yards before he slowed down and dropped the bundle. "What has my life come to?" He plunked down on the quilted bundle and buried his head in his hands.

She ached for him. How it must hurt to face the truth

she was sure he'd avoided all his life. She knelt in front of him, wrapping her hands around his. "Kingston, it isn't your fault. None of this is."

After several seconds he lifted his face and stared into her eyes. The pain in his expression drove an arrow deep into her heart.

"I wish I could believe I'd done all I could, but all I feel is defeat."

She stood up and planted her hands on her hips. "Well, get 'de feet' a-moving. We've got to set up house yet today."

He stared at her as if she'd landed in front of him from a foreign country, and then he laughed. "Now I know for sure you're crazy."

His laugh ended on a sad note; and locking hands, they walked on.

Grandpa Wells saw them first and ran to the house calling, "Mother, Mother. He's come back."

Grandma came to the door, dusting her hands on her apron. "What is it, Wes?"

"It's Harry. He's come back."

Grandma shaded her eyes. "It's Maryelle and young Kingston." She rushed toward them, Grandpa trotting after her. "You've come because of trouble." She took one look at Maryelle's face and drew her into a powder-scented hug.

Kingston stood back, awkward. She reached up for a hug. Kingston hesitated but a second, then leaned over and allowed her to wrap her arms around his neck and kiss his cheek. "It's been far too long," she said, wiping her eyes on a corner of her apron.

"We're sorry to barge in on you like this," Kingston began.

She waved him away. "I told Maryelle you'd be welcome anytime. Now you come—we'll get you set up in the bunkhouse."

Maryelle took Kingston's hand and followed, grateful Grandma didn't ask any questions. It was too fresh and upsetting to talk about.

Grandpa followed on their heels. "It's good to have young people around again. We've missed it, haven't we, Mother?"

"We have indeed. Wes, would you get me another pail of water, please? They'll need water and food to get them started."

Grandpa grabbed the pail and hurried for the pump.

Grandma chuckled. "Why, I declare. I haven't seen him with that much spring in his step in a long while. It's going to be good for him having you around."

They followed Grandma to the little house. As they stepped inside, Maryelle heard Kingston exhale as if he'd been holding his breath for a long time. "This is fine, just fine." He sounded relieved. "I can't thank you enough for lending it to us."

Grandma waved aside his thanks. "It's a pleasure. Now here's Dad with some things. Let's see what he brought."

Grandpa set a pail of water on the table and slung a sack off his shoulder to the floor. "Potatoes, a slab of bacon, some of those biscuits the young lady made, and a few other things." He reached into his pocket. "Some fresh eggs."

Grandma nodded. "That's fine, Wes. Real fine. Now

why don't we leave these young people to settle in?" She paused at the door. "I expect you're wanting some time to yourselves, but you'll no doubt be needing a few things. Come up to the house when you're ready. We have plenty of everything." She paused again and spoke over her shoulder. "Everything but someone to share it with." And then they were alone.

Maryelle stood in the center of the room, uncertain what to do next.

Kingston dropped the bundle on the bed. "Let's have a look around."

He opened the cupboard by the stove. "There are dishes and pots here. Looks like we have everything we need." He rattled the contents as he tallied them.

Maryelle pulled a chair out from the table, plopped down, buried her head in her arms, and wept.

"Maryelle?" Kingston hurried to her side, his hand stroking the back of her neck. "Don't cry, my sweet wife." He lifted her to his lap. "I suppose it was bound to come to this."

"I've taken you from your family," she sobbed.

"This is not your doing. If anyone should be blamed, it would be Dad." He pulled her head against his neck. "Besides, now we can be alone."

She sobbed harder. "I didn't want to be alone bad enough to tear your family apart."

"I don't think we were very much together in the first place."

There was enough truth in what he said for Maryelle to be soothed. "What are we going to do now?"

He stroked her cheek. "We're going to set up house-keeping here and then take it one step at a time." He sat her up. "And I suppose the first step is for me to go get the rest of our things."

The thought of him returning to his home filled her with dread. She clutched at his shoulders. "Do you have to go back?"

His green eyes intent, he gripped her shoulders and looked at her steadily. "I will not live my life in fear of his anger. I never have, and I never will." He set her on her feet. "I'll see if Grandpa Wells will let me borrow a wagon." He crossed to the door. "In the meantime you put away what we have, and"—he smiled at her, his eyes flashing warm sunshine from an ocean—"you can make something for dinner. I'm hungry."

She nodded, waiting until he left to examine the contents of the cupboard herself. A gentle peace filled her as she untied the quilt and folded Kingston's clothes into the tall wardrobe. "We'll start over," she murmured. "We'll forget about the past and start over."

By the time Kingston returned with her trunks and set them up at the end of the bed, she had thick pieces of bacon frying with sliced raw potatoes. She handed him some freshly brewed coffee while eggs cooked. "How did it go?"

"Fine. Dad was nowhere to be seen. Angus helped me. There was no one else about. He said they disappeared like shadows when we left. I hope they're thinking about how they've acted." He took a gulp of his coffee.

"This is nice," he said as she set a plate of food before him. "Just you and me." He took several mouthfuls, then added, "I'll see if I can help Grandpa Wells with anything."

"After I've cleaned up, I'll go see Grandma. She deserves some sort of explanation."

He nodded.

She took her time after dinner, loving the freedom of being on her own. Then she wandered past the garden and bushes to the house.

Grandma heard her footsteps and threw open the door before Maryelle had a chance to knock. "Come in, Child. I've gathered up some more things you'll be needing."

Maryelle gaped at the bulging sack. "You don't need to do that."

"Of course, I don't need to. I want to." She tilted her head in the general direction of the garden. "How much do you think two old people can eat? You'll be doing me a favor if you eat up some of the stuff we have stored. In fact, I was just going down to get some canned jars for you. Come along." She led the way down the narrow stairs into the dark cellar.

Maryelle waited while Grandma found a lamp and lit it.

"See what I mean?" She held the light high, and Maryelle saw row after row of filled jars—green, yellow, red, and pink.

Maryelle touched a jar. "You have enough here to feed an army."

"Crab apples, pickled crabs, plums, rhubarb sauce, beans, corn, mustard pickles, dills, sweet pickles, pickled beets, carrot pudding." Grandma touched row after row, naming the contents. "Canned chicken, canned beef." She pulled forward a jar to even out the row. "Strawberries, raspberries."

Maryelle threw up her hands, but Grandma moved on to another shelf.

"Rhubarb jam, chokecherry jelly, currant jam, carrot marmalade—"

"Grandma, what are you doing with all this stuff? Why do you do all this work for the two of you?"

Grandma gave an embarrassed laugh. "Most of it is produce from our garden and the fruit trees and bushes." She shrugged. "It seems a shame to let it waste." She smiled gently. "Besides, I enjoy doing it. Wes likes to help me." Reaching under the bottom shelf, she pulled out a flat crate. "So don't feel guilty about helping me use it up." She filled the crate with a variety of things. "Take this and feel free to help yourself." She looked at the display of filled jars. "Please."

Maryelle giggled. "It's too bad you couldn't have shipped this to London during the war. People would have given their eye teeth to be able to get stuff like this."

Grandma nodded. "When I heard about the shortages, I felt so bad. About all I could do was keep canning and hope someday it would help someone out." She patted Maryelle's shoulder. "I'm glad to help you young folk. Now let's go have a cup of tea." She waited until Maryelle carried the crate up the stairs before she blew out the lamp and followed.

Over tea, Maryelle told her of the morning's events. "I'm sure Father Brown did it, but I can't understand what he gained by destroying the garden." All her work for nothing. All the pleasure she'd enjoyed. . .

"I think it was because he knew how much it meant to you."

"I'm not sorry to be out of there, but I can't help feeling it's my fault Kingston had to leave his family."

Grandma looked thoughtful. "It seems to me the family has been falling apart for years. Kingston survived because he's strong and stubborn. I pray Angus will find the same strength."

"He seems so cowed right now."

"God has a plan in this situation. Perhaps this step is part of His plan. Who's to say? Maybe Kingston can be more effective now than he was while living there."

"Maybe." But she didn't see how. Who would step in to protect Angus with Kingston gone?

Grandma glanced over Maryelle's shoulder. "Here's Wes now and your Kingston." She rose and got two more cups as the men joined them at the table.

Kingston touched Maryelle's shoulder as he passed. She smiled at him.

"I'm glad everyone is here," Grandma began. "Because Wes and I want to propose something to you."

Maryelle didn't know what to expect and glanced at Kingston. He sat placidly waiting, but Maryelle wasn't fooled. She saw the way his eyes shifted color and knew he wondered what the Wellses had in mind.

Grandma shook her head. "Now don't go looking all fearful." She turned to Kingston. "I don't know what your plans are. Whether you plan to continue working with your father or not."

Kingston shrugged. "I don't know."

The older woman nodded. "It will take time to sort out. But Wes is finding he can't manage all the work around this place." She smiled a sweet, gentle smile at her husband. He beamed back. "The barn needs repairs; the shingles on the house need repair. There are fences to fix, the barn to clean, trees to trim." She laughed. "Lots of jobs to do." She took Grandpa's hand. "We were hoping we could hire you, at least part time."

It was a moment before Kingston answered. "I'll be pleased to help but only if it's in exchange for rent."

Grandma and Grandpa looked at each other. Grandma nodded. "We'll see."

"What do you think?" Maryelle asked later as she and Kingston sat down to supper.

"I think it's most generous, though there are definitely repairs needed around the place. I can hardly wait to get at them."

Maryelle smiled. "You're the greatest one for wanting to fix things up, aren't you?"

He nodded. "I can't stand to see things falling to rack and ruin for want of a few nails or the use of a screwdriver to tighten something."

"Then this arrangement suits you?"

"I don't want to be taking their money though. I have no idea how much they have."

"They certainly have a good supply of food." Maryelle told him about her trip to the cellar.

He pulled her to his knee and kissed her on the nose. "We'll be just fine."

"I know we will." She wrapped her arms around his neck, leaning forward for a kiss.

He pushed her back. "Now don't be distracting me while you have dishes to do."

She giggled. "It's so nice to have you to myself." She scooped up the dishes and carried them to the basin.

Kingston walked to the open door and leaned against the frame, his eyes staring far out into the distance. Maryelle followed the direction of his gaze. He was looking toward his home. She paused, her hands in the sudsy water, knowing he was troubled by the events in his family and wishing she could do something to help. She returned to scrubbing dishes. There was nothing she could do, only pray.

He turned back into the room and, grabbing a towel, dried dishes. Finished, she dumped the water on the raspberry bushes outside the door, wiped the basin, and hung it up. A strand of hair fell across her cheek. She pushed it back, tucking it in, and felt dirt on her scalp.

"My hair is full of dirt." She rubbed her fingers along her scalp.

"What did you expect? You were face down in the garden."

She wrinkled her nose. "Do you suppose I could wash it?"

His eyes flashed bright blue-green. "I'll haul water over, and you can heat it. I think I saw a tub in the little shed behind us. I'll bring it."

The tub was small, but it would serve the purpose. He hauled and heated enough water to fill it partially. She bathed, then scrubbed her hair. She leaned forward for him to pour clean water over her head.

"I'll be right back." He hurried out with the tub and returned to pile wood in the fireplace. "It's really too warm to light this, but you need to get your hair dry." He took the brush from her hand and led her to the fireplace.

She sat on the worn braided rug, leaning against his legs.

He began to lift and brush her hair. "I love your hair," he murmured, the sound of his voice sifting down through her senses.

She was more than half asleep when he put the brush aside. He lifted her and carried her to the bed.

&

A few evenings later, she pulled him from his contemplation of the far horizon. "Grandma Wells has a nice selection of books. Would you like me to read to you?"

He turned, a grin on his face. "Like in London?"

"Yes, that's what I had in mind."

"I'd love you to read to me, Mrs. Brown." His eyes darkened to the color of shadowed pines as he marched toward her, holding her gaze while he crossed to a rocking chair and pulled her to his lap. "Read away."

She took a deep breath and, opening the book, began to read.

His arms around her were warm and possessive. He rubbed a little pattern up and down her forearm. His breath smelled like the coffee he'd finished a few minutes before. He lifted his finger and tucked a bit of hair behind her ear, resting his hand on her neck.

She closed the book. "I'm so happy," she murmured. "The happiest I've been for so long."

"Me too," he said softly.

It wasn't until he left the next morning and she had the house to herself that she wondered if he was truly happy. Oh, she knew he was happy when they were kissing and hugging. But too often she caught him staring across the fields and knew he worried about his family.

ten

The days passed. Kingston worked hard at repairs on the Wells farm. And he continued to stare across the fields toward home. She could feel his concern as plainly as if it were a rock in her pocket. It seemed she could do nothing to help the situation.

"We'll ask God to show us what to do." Grandma said it over and over. Maryelle prayed too, needing God to direct their future. She had finished the breakfast dishes and opened her Bible on the table. She read a few verses, then turned to the solace of prayer.

God, I know You are almighty and powerful. You know the end from the beginning. I. . .I hardly know what this moment holds. But what I do know is this: My dear, sweet Kingston is unhappy. He's concerned about his family. He doesn't know what he should do. I don't know what I should do.

Everything in her protested at the idea of returning to the farm; yet it seemed to be the only way Kingston's needs would be met.

I don't want to go back there. Everyone was so unkind. I felt like I was waiting for a bomb to drop.

She looked around the house that was theirs for now.

It's small, God, but there're just the two of us. And I so enjoy having him to myself. But I guess You know that.

Kingston meant everything to her.

Everything? an inner voice questioned.

Enough to do what was best for him even if it meant she would have to sacrifice something? She stared at the cold fireplace, remembering how he stared out the door several times a day. She'd do anything to ease his inner torment.

She bowed her head into her hands. *I will go back if that's what he wants, but You'll have to give me the strength and wisdom to endure.*

It was two more days before she said anything to Kingston about her decision—two days in which she struggled with her reluctance—but finally she couldn't bear his staring out the door any longer.

She joined him in the open doorway, leaning against his side. He slid his hand around her shoulders.

"Why don't you go back and make your peace?"

"What do you mean?"

"I know you're missing the farm, and you're concerned about the family. Why don't you go over there and talk to your dad?" She filled her lungs with courage-giving air. "If you want to return, I'll pack up and go with you."

"Thank you, sweet brown eyes." He turned, pulling her into his arms. "But it's too soon."

She tipped her head back so she could look into his face. "What do you mean, too soon?"

He tweaked her nose. "I know my father. He has to get a lot lower before he's ready to accept what I have to say to him."

"What do you have to say to him?"

He looked past her. "I'm not sure. Which is funny because I have lots I'd like to say. Things I'd like to ask."

"Like what?"

"Why does nothing I do ever satisfy him?" He sighed. "It's always been the same. I learned to keep one eye on him and be ready to duck. He'd send me for something. 'Go get the pipe wrench,' or 'Change the wheel on that cart.' I had no idea what he meant. He wouldn't say. If I asked, he'd tell me how useless I was. But if I guessed wrong, he'd boot me." Kingston's arms tightened around her. "I hoped things would be better when I came back from the war. They weren't." He took a deep breath. "When I go back, it will be under my conditions. If he wants my help, I'll tell him what I'm prepared to do. If he doesn't"—his voice hardened—"there are still some things I'm prepared to do."

Maryelle nodded. She knew he meant Angus.

The next day she looked up to find two little girls standing outside the door. "Jeanie, Lily, how nice to see you. Come in."

Jeanie hung back uncertainly, but Lily bounded through the door. "This is your place?"

"This is where we live. What do you think of it?"

Jeanie stood in the doorway watching as Lily made a quick tour, opening cupboards, bouncing on the bed, and peering at the pictures on top of the trunk. "I like it. Don't you, Jeanie?"

The older girl nodded. "It's okay."

"How is everyone doing at home?"

Lily plopped down in one of the rockers and pumped it back and forth. "Good."

Maryelle caught the troubled look in Jeanie's face. "Jeanie, is everything all right?"

"Lena cries."

"She does?" The news startled her. Lena didn't seem the sort to cry, and she wondered if something had happened.

"Mom said it was her fault you left. Was it?"

"No, Jeanie, a lot of things happened, but it wasn't Lena's fault."

"I didn't think so. I heard Katherine tell Lena if you came back, she would be nicer this time."

Maryelle nodded, glad some positive changes had taken place but wondering how they would translate into action if Kingston decided to return.

Lily sprang from the chair. "We brought you something." She raced past Jeanie and out to a spot on the grass where she picked up a small lidded basket and carried it back to the house.

She set the basket in the middle of the floor and folded back the hinged lid. "See."

Maryelle looked inside. "A kitten. You brought me a kitten." She pulled it out and rubbed her face against the soft fur. The kitten reached up two paws and pushed at her face. Maryelle laughed.

"She's for you." Lily looked pleased with herself.

Maryelle looked from one little girl to the other. "Are you sure you want to give her away?" Two little heads bobbed up and down.

"Katherine says it's the least we can do." Jeanie looked thoughtful.

Maryelle knew at once that Jeanie was well aware of the undercurrents in the family. "Thank you both, and be sure to thank Katherine for me."

"You gonna give her a name?" Lily asked.

"I suppose I should. Unless she already has one."

Lily smiled. "I called her Rags."

"Rags. What an interesting name. Why did you call her that?"

"'Cause her fur is all mixed up like a bunch of rags."

Maryelle laughed at the description of the calico-colored kitten. "Rags it is then." She set the kitten in the basket. "We'd better close the lid so she doesn't get lost. It will take her a day or two to learn her way about. Now do you two want to go with me to find Kingston?"

"Yes!" Lily jumped up and down, speaking for both of them.

Maryelle went with them to find Kingston in the barn, fixing the frame of a small window. Grandpa Wells happily sorted a bucket of nails into smaller containers.

Kingston, looking up at her approach, saw his younger sisters and strode toward them. Lily jumped up into his arms. When Jeanie held back, he bent down and lifted her too, hugging them both and kissing their heads. "I have missed you two so much."

Lily buried her face against his neck. "You smell hot."

Jeanie clung to him.

Kingston lowered them to the ground. "Now tell me you two haven't run away from home."

Lily giggled and shook her head.

Jeanie frowned. "Of course not."

"Good. And how are Mom and Katherine and Lena?"

Jeanie said the same thing she'd said to Maryelle. "Lena cries a lot."

Kingston looked surprised. "Why does she cry?"

Jeanie stood still, ignoring the excited jumping about of her younger sister. "Mom says she's sad."

"Well, I hope she's finished being sad real soon."

Jeanie nodded.

"And Angus?"

Jeanie's eyes grew dark. "He hides."

Lily nodded. "He comes to my playhouse with me."

The muscles along Kingston's jaw bulged. He looked from one little girl to the other, then addressed Jeanie. "What do you mean, he hides? Does he hide all the time or what?"

"Only sometimes after supper."

He met Maryelle's eyes for a moment, then turned back to his sisters. "How would you like to have a glass of milk and some cookies Maryelle made?"

"Yes, please," they chorused.

After the girls had their milk and cookies and departed with the now-empty basket, leaving Rags in Maryelle's care, she turned to Kingston. "Is it time yet?"

He shook his head, his eyes dark and stormy. "Not yet."

"I don't understand. How will you know when it's time?"

"I'll know."

❧

They settled into a comfortable routine in their new surroundings. The days slipped by as Kingston did repairs and helped Mr. Wells with the garden and chores.

The much needed rain came, and the garden and crops thrived.

Under the patient direction of Grandma Wells, Maryelle learned how to can the generous bounty of the garden.

The little girls came to visit several more times. Each time they left, Kingston would stare after them, his expression thoughtful.

Each time Maryelle would ask, "Is it time?"

And he'd shake his head and answer, "Not yet."

She didn't know what he waited for, but she welcomed the delay. These days together were idyllic, and she didn't want them to end. She knew they would if Kingston made peace with his father and wanted to move back to the farm.

๑

The morning was sweet with the smell of ripe raspberries. The sky was cloudless blue, promising a warm day. Rags, having learned this was her home, sat on the step, washing herself in the sun.

"Good-for-nothing cat," Kingston growled.

Maryelle smiled at his teasing. "If you don't have a cat, you'll have mice."

"You gonna try to tell me that itty bitty thing is going to catch a mouse?" he jeered. "The way you feed her morsels from the table? Not a chance. She's already too spoiled to want to make the effort."

Maryelle grimaced. "The poor baby is hardly big enough to hunt. Give her time."

"She'll never be anything but a lap cat. Just like Sheba."

She drew herself up to her full height and planted her hands on her hips. "Sheba caught many mice in her prime, I'll have you know. Dad always said he hadn't seen a mouse in the shop from the day we got her."

He rolled his eyes.

She was about to say something silly when a figure crashed through the trees next to the house. "Someone's coming."

Kingston jerked around. "Angus."

They were both on their feet, dashing for the door.

Angus stumbled, caught a bush to slow himself, and swayed as Kingston bounded to his side, Maryelle hard on his heels. She gasped at the sight of him—a huge welt beside his eye, his lips pouring out blood, tears and blood mingled together dripping from his chin.

"Bring him inside," she ordered.

Kingston led the boy to a rocker and pushed him down.

Maryelle grabbed a basin of water and a clean rag and knelt at his side; but when she reached out her hand to sponge his face, he shrank back.

"It's all right," she murmured. "I won't hurt you. I only want to clean up your face."

His eyes round with fear, he let her sponge away the blood and dirt.

Maryelle bit down hard to keep from saying something about the bruises.

Kingston ground out the words. "Angus, what happened?"

Angus lifted tortured eyes to his brother. A sob caught in his throat. "I did what you said. I pretended I wasn't afraid. I said, 'I'm not afraid of you. You can't hurt me.'" His voice dropped to a whisper.

Kingston groaned. "I only meant you shouldn't let him make you afraid inside. Challenging him like that was like waving a red flag in front of him." He slammed a fist into his palm and muttered, "It's time." He strode for the door, pausing to speak to Angus. "You stay here with Maryelle. I'm going to see our father."

He jumped off the step, grabbed a thick branch off the ground, and slammed it against a tree. "It's time!" he shouted, swinging the club as he strode toward the farm.

Maryelle's heart thudded like a galloping horse as she stared after him.

Angus's moaning drew her attention back to him.

Rags trotted into the house and, seeing a lap waiting, jumped to Angus's knee. Angus cradled the kitten to his chest, his eyes shining with tears.

She studied his bruised face and thought she detected dark hollows under his eyes, evidence of many days of strain. "You look about all in. Why don't you lie down and rest?"

His gaze strayed to the bed, but all he did was tighten up into a little ball.

"Go ahead. Looks like Rags would be glad to keep you company."

He wrapped his arms protectively around the kitten.

"You'll have the place to yourself. I'll be outside picking raspberries."

Finally he kicked off his boots and dropped to the bed, Rags cradled in the crook of his arm.

She slipped out, pulling the door partway shut.

Although there were berries to be picked, she didn't go to the raspberry bushes. Instead she stood at the far tree, staring in the direction of the farm, praying Kingston would be safe.

She pressed her fist to her mouth, determined not to

cry. She had never been so afraid, not even during the war when a zeppelin had flown over London. Not even when Kingston had gone to the front lines.

She had seen this enemy. She had tasted her own fear.

She returned to check on Angus. He'd fallen into an uneasy sleep from which he occasionally cried out. She pulled a quilt over his shoulders and went back out. Her restlessness would not be cured until Kingston returned.

Finally he crested the hill, too far away for her to see his face. As she ran toward him, a sob caught in the back of her throat.

"Kingston, are you all right?"

He smiled down at her, then draped his arm around her shoulder. "I'm just fine. How's Angus?"

"Sound asleep with Rags curled up in his arms."

"Best thing for the boy." He glanced down at her. "Do you mind if he stays with us a few days?"

"Of course I don't mind." She pulled away from his grasp and gave him a hard look. "But you better tell me what happened over there." She ran her gaze down his full length, then checked behind him. "You didn't hit him, did you?"

Kingston snorted. "I've never hit him in my life. I don't intend to start now."

"You roared out of here in such a rage, that huge stick in your hand. I feared you would strike him."

Kingston pulled her back to his side. "Mom was waiting for me when I got there and insisted she was going with me. I was concerned about that. I didn't need anything to fuel Dad's anger. She said she would stay out of the way until I said my piece, but she wanted to say something too and said she needed me there to give her strength." Kingston stopped walking.

Maryelle knew he was mentally back at the farm, reliving the whole thing.

"I found him beating the rake to bits with a sledge hammer."

She gasped. "He didn't come after you, did he?"

"No. I wouldn't have let him. I told him to put the sledge down so we could talk. He swung it a few more times to let me know who was boss, then muttered something about 'that's done' and wiped his brow, making a big show of how hard he'd been working. Truth was, he was only venting his rage.

"He turned to me and said, 'I suppose that young pup has gone whimpering to you.'

"I didn't even bother answering. I said, 'I told you if you ever hit Angus again, you'd have me to deal with and I meant it.'

"He glowered at me, but I never paid mind.

"'Angus will be staying with me,' I told him, 'until we can work out some agreement.'"

"He started muttering about the boy being underage and I'd better watch myself if I thought I could interfere with a father's discipline. I was about to tell him I didn't care about any of that when Mom stepped forward practically toe to toe with him. Bold as can be. She said, 'I lost one boy to your fearsome behavior. I'll not be losing another. You do whatever Kingston asks. I want Angus back here. And I want him safe.'

"He stared at her so hard I thought his eyes would explode out of his head." Kingston laughed. "In all my life I've never seen Mom stand up to Dad. But I'm telling you, when she finally got up the guts to do it, she did it right proud."

"About time, I'd say." Maryelle couldn't help thinking it was too bad she hadn't stepped in on Kingston's behalf.

"Better late than never." His voice deepened. "Maybe it will do some good for Angus."

"But then what happened?" Nothing had been resolved. Just a lot of words exchanged.

"That was it. I said Angus would be here and I'd be waiting for Dad to make up his mind that Angus would go home on my terms, not his."

"Well." Maryelle stopped dead and pulled away. "I guess that means Angus is about to become a permanent guest."

He stared at her, a puzzled look on his face. "Why do you say that?"

"Because I can't see your father changing."

"Ah. But you forget something. He now has no sons there to help him, and there's a pile of work to be done. There's more hay to cut and stack, and soon enough it will be time to harvest the grain. Don't think that won't occur to him. You wait and see. He'll be marching down the road soon enough, begging us all to come home."

Maryelle turned away. No doubt Kingston was right, but the thought of returning gave her no pleasure. No pleasure at all.

They made a bed for Angus in the little shop behind their house. He took his meals with them and followed Kingston around all day, helping with repairs.

❧

"I don't see any reason not to cut that stand of hay behind the corrals," Kingston said.

They were gathered in the bigger house having a mid-morning break.

Grandma Wells nodded. "What do you think, Wes?"

"Sounds fine. Just fine." He downed the last of his tea in one gulp and stood. "Let's get at it." He tromped out. Kingston and Angus trailed after him.

"That young man is looking happier every day," Grandma commented. "Why, I believe I saw him smile this morning."

Maryelle agreed. "He no longer ducks his head every time I look at him."

"It's good for him to be with you and Kingston."

"Seems to be." She watched the men checking over the ancient equipment Grandpa owned. It was fourteen days since Angus had staggered in, his face bleeding and his heart about to burst. Fourteen days and not a word from Father Brown. Perhaps her prediction would prove correct. Not that she didn't like Angus, but she missed having Kingston to herself. Seemed now he was always busy talking to Angus or playing catch with him or something.

Grandma patted her hand. "It's a hard time for you, but don't forget God is working things out. He sees your need as well as He sees what Angus needs. You wait and be patient. Your father-in-law will be coming round soon enough."

That evening Kingston and Angus played another game of catch.

Angus threw the ball harder than usual, and Kingston missed it, grumbling at the way his younger brother made him work so hard.

Angus laughed out loud.

Maryelle stared at the boy. It was the first time she'd heard him laugh—a laugh that sounded much like Kingston's.

At fifteen, she had laughed about everything. She couldn't imagine what it would be like to be afraid to laugh. She was suddenly ashamed of her eagerness to see the boy sent home.

She went outside. "Come on, Angus. I'll help you. Sort of even out the balance."

Angus stopped. His smile disappeared, but she grabbed the ball from his hands and raced away. "Move out, Angus. We'll outfox him. Come on, Kingston. See if you can get the ball from us."

Angus backed away, leaving Kingston in the open. Kingston dove at Maryelle, but she chucked the ball at Angus. Kingston turned abruptly and made a leap for Angus. Maryelle tackled Kingston from behind, bringing him to the ground.

Angus pointed and jeered. "You fell like a rock." He laughed. "The bigger they are, the harder they fall." He pranced up and down, laughing.

Kingston sat back on his heels, grinning at the boy. He met Maryelle's gaze. She knew how much pleasure he got from seeing his brother laugh. It sounded good, she admitted. And it felt good to have had a part in changing this boy from a somber, fearful lad to this boisterous, laughing one.

Kingston pulled her to his side. "I wonder how long it's been since he's felt free to laugh?"

"No matter how long it's been, it's too long. When I think how much I laughed at his age." She shook her head.

"What are you two whispering about?" Angus demanded.

"None of your beeswax." Kingston jerked his head away in a dismissive gesture.

"You think not? Well, I'm about to make it my business." He raced around the pair of them and grabbed Kingston from behind.

Maryelle jumped out of the way as Kingston pulled the boy over his head and the two tussled on the ground, grunting and laughing.

Finally Kingston pinned the younger boy to the ground. "You are getting too big for your britches, young one. You be careful, or I'll have to turn you over my knee."

Angus sobered.

Kingston stood, pulling him to his feet. "Angus." His voice was full of misery. "I was only teasing. I would never hit you. You know that."

Angus nodded. "How long before he makes me go home?"

"Angus, I promise you aren't going home until I have a few promises from Dad. Promises that I will make certain he keeps." His expression grew hard. "I have a few aces up my sleeve yet. So don't you be worrying."

He draped one arm around his younger brother's shoulders and pulled Maryelle close on his other side. "Now how about some milk and cookies before we go to bed?"

❧

Two days later, Maryelle glanced up to see Katherine

standing a few feet from the house.

"Hello, Katherine. Come in and visit." She hoped she had successfully disguised her surprise. Her mouth grew dry as she thought of the possible reasons for this visit.

eleven

"Is there anything the matter?" she asked the girl.

Katherine stepped a little closer. "I have a message for Kingston."

"Come in and sit while I get him." She waved toward a chair and smiled as the girl entered the room, walking as if stepping on eggs. "Kingston is out back. I'll call him." She leaned out the window. "Kingston, Katherine's here to see you." He thrust his head out from under a branch he'd been trimming, his eyes wide with curiosity. A few feet away, Angus poked his head out, the fear in his eyes as plain to see as the pine needles stuck in his hair. "Come on in. I'll set out some cookies."

And so the four of them sat around the table, as awkward as strangers sharing a table on the train.

"Dad said he wants you to come home." Katherine kept her face averted.

"That all he said?" Kingston asked.

"What he said was, 'Go tell your brother to get on home.'"

She shrugged. "Guess he never even said which brother." Her glance darted to Angus. "I thought he meant you." She turned back to Kingston. "I suppose you should come too."

Kingston held up a hand. "I'll go. Angus, you stay here until I talk to Dad. Come on, Katherine." He hesitated.

"Unless you want to stay and visit."

"Please do," Maryelle begged. "I'd like that." Perhaps she and Katherine could learn to be friends if Lena was absent.

Katherine nodded.

"I'll be back soon." Kingston kissed Maryelle. Rags bounded in as he left.

Angus scooped up the kitten. "Recognize this kitten?"

Katherine took a good look. "Is it one of Mitten's batch?"

"Yup. Lily brought her over and gave her to Maryelle. I tell you this is the way a cat should be treated. Hand-fed from the table, sleeps on the bed—" He grinned at Maryelle, repeating words he'd heard Kingston say as he teased her. Maryelle couldn't help thinking the same words could well apply to Angus himself.

Katherine laughed at her younger brother. "Sounds like a nice way to live."

Maryelle smiled at the pair. "It's so nice to have you both here."

Katherine gave her a sober look. "You aren't mad at me?"

"Of course not. I'd like us to be friends."

"Me too." Then Katherine turned back to Angus, and they played with the cat.

Maryelle paid them only half a mind, her thoughts on Kingston and the task that lay ahead of him. She prayed so hard that she didn't even hear him return until he stood in the doorway.

"Kingston." She ran to greet him.

Angus left off the game he and Katherine were playing and waited.

"We worked out an agreement." He kissed her nose and pulled her inside. "Sit down. I'll tell you all about it."

Katherine stood. "I best be getting home."

"You might as well hear this too. It's bound to affect you."

She sat down obediently.

"Dad and I reached an agreement." He turned to Angus. "You'll be going home. He'll not hit you again. If it ever happens again, you'll be living with us. I agreed to work for him on that condition."

Maryelle swallowed hard. Despite her resolve to return for Kingston's sake and with God's help, it vanished in the light of reality. She drew a deep breath and prayed for strength.

Kingston reached across the table and took her hand. "Part time only, and he agreed to pay me wages."

She gaped at him. "Part time?" What would he do the rest of the time? How would they survive on part-time wages?

"I won't be able to spare him anything more. This place will take some building up again."

"What place?"

"Grandma and I have been talking. Grandpa can't manage any longer. She asked if I would consider buying the place from them. I'm going to do it."

Stunned silence greeted his statement.

"Angus, you'll stay here tonight. We'll go across tomorrow." He grinned at Maryelle. "By the way, we're invited for supper tomorrow night."

Later, when Katherine had left for home and Angus had

gone to his bed in the little shack, Maryelle finally had a chance to ask all the questions barging through her mind.

"What makes you think your father will keep his end of the agreement?" She pulled the pins from her hair and shook it free.

He tipped back in his chair, his eyes bright as the water and sky and warm with love. "Because, my sweet brown eyes, I made it clear that if he ever hit Angus again, he would find himself without any help. He could never manage on his own, and he knows it."

She shook her head.

"Besides, if he can control his temper when he's ashamed for someone to see how he acts, he can control it because he doesn't like the consequences."

"I hope you're right."

He caught her arm and pulled her to his knee. "If I'm not, then I walk away and take Angus with me. I'd like to hope he will change; but unless he lets God work in his life, I don't see it happening. In the meantime he'll comply out of necessity." He paused a moment. "I always wondered about Mom. Today she told me she'd shoved aside her faith in order to keep the peace. But now she says she'll do what's right even if Dad doesn't like it. I think Dad knows when he's run into overwhelming odds."

"You never said anything to me about buying this farm."

"I needed to think about it. I didn't want you to get your hopes up until I was sure what I was going to do. I didn't make up my mind until I walked over to the farm. Suddenly everything fell into place."

"I'm glad we're going to stay. I like it here."

"As much as you like this?" He drew her near so he could kiss her.

"Umm."

When he would have pulled away, she held him close. He chuckled low in his chest.

After a minute or two, he pushed away. "I thought I would never enjoy another farm the way I did ours." He jerked his head in the direction of home. "But I discovered it's the work I enjoy. I've grown to love this place. There's so much I want to do."

"I confess I didn't want to go back to living with your family again."

"I figured that out." He kissed her nose. "But thank you for being willing."

"I worried, too, what would happen to Grandpa if we left."

"Me too."

"Seems like God has provided an answer for everyone's need."

"He has promised to meet all our needs."

Rags jumped up on Maryelle's lap, purring and pushing against her arm, begging for attention. Maryelle shoved her away. "Not now, Rags," she murmured. There was no room for the cat as she hugged Kingston.

❧

Angus hung back as they approached the house. Maryelle shot him a look of sympathy. She wasn't looking forward to this either. It was only for Kingston's sake she was willing to enter this house again.

"Come on, you two. No one's going to bite." He chuckled. "You both look like you're about to enter a bear's den."

Angus smiled sheepishly.

"Lead on." Maryelle clung to Kingston's arm. "I'm ready."

They mounted the steps, Angus on their heels, and stepped into the kitchen. Familiar smells met them—the smell of warm milk, roast chicken, fresh bread, and spicy applesauce.

Mother Brown turned from the stove. "Come on in. Supper's almost ready." Her gaze found Angus practically glued to Kingston's back, and she smiled. "Welcome home, Son."

Maryelle's jaw dropped open. Never had she known Mother Brown to appear so happy to see someone. For a moment, anger blazed through her veins. Why couldn't she have welcomed Kingston like this? Why not her even? But she couldn't stay angry; Kingston had gained what he wanted—peace in his family. An uncertain, untried peace. As for loving him, she would take care of that so he would never miss not having it from his family.

Father Brown thudded up the steps.

Angus shifted to Kingston's side. "You've no need to be afraid," Kingston murmured.

Their father stepped into the room. "I see you're here in good time."

"Wouldn't be late for one of Mom's meals." He held out his hand. For a moment his father stared at it; then he gave a hard squeeze. "How have you been?" Kingston asked.

"Not bad considering how much work I've got to do."

Kingston nodded. "I'll be over in the morning to help."

The little girls bounded through the door and gave Kingston a hug. When Maryelle bent down to hug them, Lily wrapped her arms around Maryelle's neck. "I love you," she whispered.

Tears blurred her vision as Maryelle whispered back, "I love you too."

Jeanie allowed herself to be hugged; and when Maryelle whispered the same words in her ear, the child's eyes grew wide.

Katherine came down the stairs. "Hi," she said, smiling shyly.

Lena followed her, carefully avoiding Maryelle's gaze.

The meal was delicious and the conversation almost relaxed as Kingston told about the work he'd been doing and stories of Rags's mischief.

After the meal, the men went outside. "To check on what we'll be doing tomorrow," Kingston said.

Lena ducked back up the stairs as Maryelle helped the little girls clear the table. In a few minutes, Lena returned, her hands behind her back, and sidled up to Maryelle.

"Here." She thrust an object into Maryelle's hand.

Maryelle looked down. "It's my picture of Sheba."

"I took it one day when I was feeling spiteful. I'm sorry."

"I'm just glad you returned it. Thank you." Before she could change her mind, she gave Lena a quick hug. "I hope we can be friends now."

Lena hung her head. "It was never really you I was mad at." She shrugged. "I guess it was the war. You see, my boyfriend died over there."

"I'm so sorry."

She nodded. "Mom talked to me about it and said I had to let go of my bad feelings. I'm trying not to be so angry." She shook her head. "But it's hard."

"It will take time."

Lena nodded, then turned to put away the dishes Jeanie had dried.

Kingston returned. "Shall we be going home, Mrs. Brown?"

She nodded. "I'm ready."

Hand in hand, they walked back over the hills, pausing at the last rise for one more look at his family home.

Kingston pulled Maryelle into his arms. "I could not imagine I would ever be this happy." He kissed the top of her head. "Your love has made my life complete."

"Thank you, Mr. Canada. I love you too. But we need to thank God for the way He's worked everything out."

" 'All things work together for good to them that love God.' Never before has that verse meant so much. Indeed God has done marvelous things."

"I know." She turned to look up into his face. "Will everything be okay now?"

He smiled. "It's a beginning. I'm sure there'll be ups and downs along the way." He hugged her close. "But God will be with us each step of the way."

She wrapped her arms around his waist. "Let's go home."

It felt so good to have a place of their own and to know Kingston could help his family at the same time. Her heart felt full and content.

A Letter To Our Readers

Dear Reader:

In order that we might better contribute to your reading enjoyment, we would appreciate your taking a few minutes to respond to the following questions. We welcome your comments and read each form and letter we receive. When completed, please return to the following:

Fiction Editor
Heartsong Presents
PO Box 719
Uhrichsville, Ohio 44683

1. Did you enjoy reading *Maryelle* by Linda Ford?
   ❏ Very much! I would like to see more books by this author!
   ❏ Moderately. I would have enjoyed it more if

   _____

   _____

   _____

2. Are you a member of **Heartsong Presents**? ❏ Yes ❏ No
   If no, where did you purchase this book? _____

   _____

3. How would you rate, on a scale from 1 (poor) to 5 (superior), the cover design? _____

4. On a scale from 1 (poor) to 10 (superior), please rate the following elements.

   ____ Heroine   ____ Plot
   ____ Hero   ____ Inspirational theme
   ____ Setting   ____ Secondary characters

5. These characters were special because?_____

_____

_____

6. How has this book inspired your life?_____

_____

_____

7. What settings would you like to see covered in future
   Heartsong Presents books? _____

_____

_____

8. What are some inspirational themes you would like to see
   treated in future books? _____

_____

_____

9. Would you be interested in reading other **Heartsong
   Presents** titles? ❏ Yes ❏ No

10. Please check your age range:
    ❏ Under 18   ❏ 18-24
    ❏ 25-34   ❏ 35-45
    ❏ 46-55   ❏ Over 55

Name_____

Occupation _____

Address _____

City_____ State_____ Zip_____

KEY WEST

Visit the historical port of Key West—accessible only by boat—along with an intriguing cast characters from North America and the Caribbean. Share in their search for refuge and hope as they begin new lives on this eight-square-mile island.

Battling forces of nature, human enemies, and their own powerful emotions, four women make their home where Florida meets the sea in wild tropical beauty. Join them on an emotional journey through time to see if faith and love can endure the rough waves of life.

Historical, paperback, 480 pages, 5 ³/₁₆" x 8"

♥ ♥ ♥ ♥ ♥ ♥ ♥ ♥ ♥❤ ♥ ♥ ♥ ♥ ♥ ♥ ♥ ♥

♥ ♥ ♥ ♥ ♥ ♥ ♥ ♥ ♥❤ ♥ ♥ ♥ ♥ ♥ ♥ ♥ ♥

Heart❤ong

------- **Presents** -------

Great Inspirational Romance at a Great Price!

Heartsong Presents books are inspirational romances in contemporary and historical settings, designed to give you an enjoyable, spirit-lifting reading experience. You can choose wonderfully written titles from some of today's best authors like Peggy Darty, Sally Laity, Tracie Peterson, Colleen L. Reece, Debra White Smith, and many others.

When ordering quantities less than twelve, above titles are $3.25 each.
Not all titles may be available at time of order.

ℋEARTSONG ♥ PRESENTS

Love Stories Are Rated G!

That's for godly, gratifying, and of course, great! If you love a thrilling love story but don't appreciate the sordidness of some popular paperback romances, **Heartsong Presents** is for you. In fact, **Heartsong Presents** is the premiere inspirational romance book club featuring love stories where Christian faith is the primary ingredient in a marriage relationship.

Sign up today to receive your first set of four, never-before-published Christian romances. Send no money now; you will receive a bill with the first shipment. You may cancel at any time without obligation, and if you aren't completely satisfied with any selection, you may return the books for an immediate refund!

Imagine. . .four new romances every four weeks—two historical, two contemporary—with men and women like you who long to meet the one God has chosen as the love of their lives. . .all for the low price of $10.99 postpaid.

To join, simply complete the coupon below and mail to the address provided. **Heartsong Presents** romances are rated G for another reason: They'll arrive Godspeed!

YES! Sign me up for Hearts♥ng!

NEW MEMBERSHIPS WILL BE SHIPPED IMMEDIATELY!
Send no money now. We'll bill you only $10.99 postpaid with your first shipment of four books. Or for faster action, call toll free 1-800-847-8270.

NAME _____

ADDRESS _____

CITY_____STATE _____ ZIP_____

MAIL TO: HEARTSONG PRESENTS, P.O. Box 721, Uhrichsville, Ohio 44683
or visit www.heartsongpresents.com